Moving On with Mr. Fix It

HELEN WALTON

Walton House Publishing

Contents

Chapter One

The phone rang out with an annoying beep. Once again, my estranged husband refused to answer my call. I slid my phone into my shorts pocket and stared across the deck at the beauty of the beach.

Surfers danced across the sapphire blue waves of Hope Bay. They appeared so free and happy. I longed for their freedom. If only I was brave enough to try my new surfboard in the water.

The warm, salty breeze blew in like a soft lover's caress against my cheek, along with the late summer sunshine dancing up my arms. There was nothing I didn't like about living in Hope Bay. In fact, I loved it. I should have moved here years ago when I'd known for certain my marriage wouldn't last.

"Madeline, are you out back?" called Hannah.

"Yes, on the deck." My quiet morning was about to be shattered. Not by my sister—she was great—but by her dog, Bosco the beagle.

A creak of the timber decking and Hannah rounded the corner on the wraparound veranda of my new abode with Bosco by her side on a long leash. Thank goodness he was on a leash. After Katie told us of her disastrous dog-sitting fiasco while we'd been on a cruise, I'd made myself a promise to keep Bosco on a leash if I dog-sat him. At all times.

"Thanks for watching Bosco this weekend." Hannah bent down and patted his tan, black, and white head.

She straightened and handed me the leash. Bosco tilted his head to the side. His big, brown eyes took on a pleading quality. He was adorable, and he loved Hannah unconditionally. If only men loved like that. It sure would make life easier.

"Have a good time at the writers' conference."

"I'll try to, but I'll worry about this guy."

"He'll be fine." I patted Bosco's head, his soft fur smooth under my fingers.

"If I wasn't the key speaker, I'd stay home."

She twirled the length of her dark russet auburn hair around her finger. I wished I'd been as lucky as her in the hair color department. Mine was brick red.

"Go enjoy your success. You deserve it with how hard you work."

"I'm lucky to have you." She dropped her hair. "Don't suppose you'll go halves with me in your custard slice?"

"No." I loved my sister, but sharing sweets? I dropped my gaze to the pastry plated on the table. My mouth watered at the sight awaiting my hungry taste buds. I could almost taste the sweet, creamy pastry now. "I've been waiting all week for my treat. Besides, you don't want to drop icing sugar all over your gorgeous black pantsuit, do you?"

Madeline glanced down in longing at the pastry, then at her outfit. "I suppose not." She sighed. "Bailey makes the best pastries in the whole of Western Australia. Scratch that, the whole of Australia."

"And she makes low-fat ones too."

"Lucky for both of us." Hannah patted her stomach. "Otherwise, this would be huge by now."

I snorted. Hannah wasn't huge. "I've lost a few kilos since moving here. It must be all the fresh air and exercise, plus getting this house ready to open as a bed-and-breakfast."

"When is the contractor coming to quote the exterior?"

"Today." I sipped my glass of iced coffee, another of my weekly indulgences.

"I should stay. You'll be busy, and Bosco will get underfoot."

"Hannah, go. I'll manage."

She gave me a tight smile. "Keep his leash on when outside and you won't have the same disaster as Katie."

"I will, and I have no chocolate inside the house, so we're safe on that front too."

"I still can't believe he almost died from eating chocolate cake." She ruffled Bosco's ears.

The beagle lapped up the attention and rolled over for a belly rub, with his paws dangling in mid-air. Hannah obliged his cute demand.

"Funny how Katie and Joel were busy this weekend when I mentioned the conference."

"She kicked him under the table." I snickered.

"I spotted her kick him, too." Hannah stood. "They're so great together. Will we hear wedding bells soon?"

"Hard to say." I rolled my shoulders. "She loves Joel—any idiot can see they're happy and in love—but Garry and me separating hurt her."

"You stayed together for as long as possible." Hannah dropped a hand to my shoulder and squeezed.

"I tried." A small sigh left my lungs. "I really did."

"Why hasn't Garry signed the joint divorce application papers?"

Shrugging, I rubbed the frown from my brow. I didn't understand Garry either.

"Strange, since he's the one who cheated." She let go of my shoulder. "I guess some relationships aren't meant to last. Now, you can find one that will."

I shook my head. "Another relationship is the last thing on my mind. What with the bed-and-breakfast makeover, I wouldn't have the time or energy. I'll leave the romances to you to write in your books. How long until I can read your new story?"

"Don't ask." She pouted.

"That bad?"

"I've lost my spark." She waved her hands in the air. "Hopefully, the conference will help me find inspiration again."

"I'm sure you will," I said, standing and hugging her. "Now, get out of here; you've got a crowd of romance writers to dazzle with your brilliance."

"Thanks." She beamed, more confident than a moment ago.

"That's what big sisters are for."

Hannah turned and left the way she'd come, her curly hair swishing with her steps. The timber boards creaked under her footfalls again. The weather had worn away the paint until it flaked and peeled like the place was ancient when it wasn't. I couldn't wait for the contractor to give me a quote for bringing the once former grand two-story house back to life. A lick of paint would see the house right. The interior was fine, but the constant pound of saltwater and sand had damaged the exterior.

I sat back in my chair, causing the cane to squeak, and patted Bosco's head. His ears were soft, like velvet. He rolled his eyes back in enjoyment. It took his mind off Hannah leaving, and we both gazed at the beach in longing. The surfers once again drew my gaze as they frolicked across the swell of the waves.

A flock of seagulls converged over the sand, their white and grey plumes shadowing the sky-blue horizon, dragging my gaze in their direction. The birds landed at the feet of a family of tourists eating on the beach. Big mistake. The seagulls surrounded them. The little girl squealed and flapped her arms. Bosco barked in excitement. The birds flapped their wings. Bosco barked a high-pitched yelp and tugged on his leash.

"Calm down, Bosco."

The boy ran at the seagulls, his towel trailing behind him like a cape. The birds took flight. Bosco yanked his leash harder. My chair scooted a few centimeters on the timber decking, screeching like nails down a blackboard. The boy continued chasing the birds, heading straight toward us.

Bosco barked excited yips. The birds flew closer and up over our heads. Bosco jumped into the air, yanking me forward with the jerk on the leash, and knocked over the cane table. The custard slice flew through the air and landed on my face. I wiped it away but smeared the thick creamy filling over my cheeks and into my eyes, making it impossible to see.

The leash jerked tighter in my hand, but I held on for dear life. There was no way I'd let go of the leash when I wouldn't see where Bosco ran. The chair scooted across the timber decking again. This time, the chair kept going. I stood, but Bosco had wrapped the leash around my legs, and I fell back into the chair.

"Are you kidding me?"

Hannah had left five minutes ago, and Bosco was already causing trouble.

Bosco dragged the chair and me further across the deck. I smacked into something semi-solid. It creaked with an ominous portent of disaster. Was it the guardrail? I flung my hands out to grab onto something, anything, but they only met air. The chair tilted backward on two legs. I pinwheeled my arms but kept falling.

"Ah," I squawked, much like the seagulls' moments before.

"Easy there, I've got you," said a deep baritone voice as strong hands gripped my shoulders.

The man's voice was electrifying. He'd halted my fall in mid-air. My heart beat a wild tempo in my chest from the almost catastrophe. There was also a small jump in my heart because I liked the sound of his voice and the pressure of his firm hands on my shoulders. My skin reacted in a tingle I felt all the way to my toes.

"Th...anks," I babbled.

"You seem to be in a bit of a mess."

I laughed. "Since I can't see, I'll take your word for it."

He chuckled. His warm breath puffed over the side of my neck, making my insides clench.

I cleared my throat. "Is Bosco all right?"

"If you're talking about the beagle licking the food from the deck, then I'd say yes."

"Yes, that'd be him. Would you mind helping me up or letting me down slowly?"

"No problem."

A second later, he lifted me onto the deck. Solid thumps thudded behind me, sounding like he'd jumped onto the deck. Then the chair skidded along the deck as he thrust the chair away from the edge.

"There you go. Got anything to wipe your face?" he asked.

His voice did exciting things to my body. What did he look like? I shouldn't even care, but when a voice sounded as intoxicating as his, then I could only imagine he was as stunning as the voice that kept whispering over my skin in a caress that sent my heart skipping.

"Ah." I hesitated. I could ask him to go in the back door and fetch a tea towel or paper towel, but I didn't want a stranger in my house. Call me old-fashioned, or just old. Forty-two wasn't old in some people's eyes.

He pressed a soft cloth to my face. I inhaled the tangy masculine aroma of his deodorant and the scent of the man. It'd been too long since I'd been this close to the heady aroma. Too long since I'd... I licked my lips. The custard filling slid into my mouth. The sweetness added to my heightened overwrought senses. Would he taste as sweet? Since when did I think about tasting men?

I fumbled for the cloth and hastily wiped the rest of my face. The sooner I handed him back his rag, the better. Then he would leave, and I wouldn't experience any of these ridiculous butterflies fluttering in my stomach. I tried opening my eyes, but it was like glue had stuck my eyelashes together.

"Now I can see your pretty face and gorgeous brown eyes," the man cooed.

Now, wait a minute. Who did he think he was, coming on to a stranger? I might have had thoughts, but I hadn't voiced them, and sure, he'd rescued me, but...

I forced my eyes open, ready to tell him pickup lines like those didn't work on grown women.

The words stuck in my throat.

The man, or Adonis, held Bosco's face between his bronzed hands. He wasn't even looking at me. Of course, he wasn't talking about me. What was I thinking? No one as good-looking as him would call me pretty or gorgeous.

I'd call him those, though, even with his rough ruggedness. His thick, dark brown hair sat just below his shoulders and matched his short, trimmed beard. The reflective sunglasses hid his eyes, but nothing hid his body. His gorgeous body of bronzed skin, smooth, tight muscles, and a spattering of dark chest hair. On his right bicep swirled an equally gorgeous tattoo in black and grey patterns. He patted Bosco's head. Each movement made the muscles and veins in his forearms shift in a hypnotizing way.

He must be a surfer with his looks and *that* body. The body of a man, not like most of the younger surfers I'd observed at the beach. No, he was a gorgeous man, someone out of one of Hannah's romance novels. Yes, that had to be it. I'd hallucinated him or dreamed about him.

The man unclicked Bosco's leash.

"Wait!" I jerked out of my stupor.

Both heads turned my way.

"Don't let him go! He'll run away."

He turned back to Bosco. "Bit of a naughty boy, are you?"

"You have no idea." I sighed and waved my hand at the mess on my deck. "This happened five minutes after his owner left. I think he suffers from separation anxiety."

"He's not yours?"

"No, he's my sister's dog."

"Ah." He held on to Bosco's collar. "I'll untangle you, then clip the leash back on, okay?"

I glanced down at the tangled mess of the leash around my legs, tying me to the chair. "Oh, okay."

He stepped closer. His masculine scent wafted. The same aroma I'd sniffed on the cloth. I squinted at the cloth in my hands. Not a cloth, his T-shirt. Which I'd ruined with my custard slice and makeup smeared across the white fabric. Could this get any more embarrassing?

He unwound the leash from my legs and chair. His fingers accidentally skimmed my left ankle and sent a jolt of awareness up my leg. Yep, I'd read way too many romance books. Grown women didn't experience these sorts of things with strangers.

I licked my lips and stood. "Thanks."

He clicked Bosco's leash onto his collar and handed me the loop. Another accidental touch of his fingers and another jolt of awareness zoomed through my body. Was instant attraction like this real?

"You're welcome, Madeline."

I frowned. How does he know my name?

"I'm sorry, do I know you?"

"No." He tugged on the loops of his shorts.

My gaze dropped to his hands, to the expanse of bronzed, firm abdominal muscles, and then snapped back to his face when I realized I was still checking him out.

"I'm Nate. Nate Hudson from Hudson Construction. I'm here to give you a quote."

Oh, shit. I'd checked out my soon-to-be employee.

Chapter Two

The day kept getting worse. I crinkled his T-shirt into one hand and held out my other hand.

"Sorry about your top."

His muscular, bronzed arm stretched forward, and his palm clasped mine as he shook my hand. A jolt of awareness zapped between our palms so powerful I imagined swooning into his arms.

"The spoils of rescuing a damsel in distress." His lips spread into a sexy smirk.

Heat worked its way into my cheeks.

Don't blush. You look like a beetroot when you blush.

Pushing every ounce of professionalism to the surface, I said, "Thanks again for the rescue. I'll wash your T-shirt and get it back to you."

"Are you giving me the job without a quote?"

"No," I scoffed.

He slid his sunglasses off his face and hooked them into the back pocket of his shorts. Now the full effect of his gorgeousness assaulted my senses. His eyes were a deep and mysterious green, but there were crinkles of smile lines at the edges of his eyes showing he smiled and laughed a great deal.

"Good." He walked over to the broken guardrail and inspected the structure. "I'd say the entire guardrail needs replacing going by this broken section."

I straightened and brushed aside my embarrassment. Time to prove I'm a capable businesswoman. Not an idiot for letting a dog cause havoc.

"Yes. I'd like you to inspect the whole exterior and quote all repairs. I'd also like the exterior of the house painted."

"What about inside the house? Anything you'd like quoted in there?"

"Surprisingly, the former owners kept up the inside, not the outside. I may hang new curtains and match them to the new bedspreads before I open."

"Open?" He folded his arms over his naked chest.

My gaze dipped to the bulge of his folded biceps and the swirling pattern of his tattoo. My finger itched to trace the line to figure out the image.

"I'm converting the house into a bed-and-breakfast. I'd hoped to have it finished before summer, but the settlement took longer than I expected."

More like it took my husband longer to settle our agreement and buy me out of my share of our silk farm. At least it was one thing finished between us, even though I was still waiting for Garry to sign the joint divorce application papers. I didn't understand what was taking him so long. He had another woman in his life. I could submit a form by myself, but we went into this marriage together and I believed we should end it together.

"How many bedrooms are there?"

"Six in total. There's one bedroom downstairs, which is mine, and the other bedrooms upstairs will be for the guests apart from one which is my daughter's until she's ready to leave. Which wouldn't surprise me if it was soon," I babbled. *Why am I babbling? Does he have to be topless?* I wrung the top in my hands, wishing he'd put it back on so all his naked skin wasn't drawing my attention.

"What about your husband?"

"We're no longer together." I pursed my lips. Why was I telling this stranger and potential employee about my personal life? "Anyway, would you mind doing a quote while I head inside and wash off this mess?"

The sooner I got away from my obsessive ogling, the better.

"Go right ahead. I'll be out here when you're finished."

"Come on, Bosco." I tugged his leash, but he wouldn't budge. I glared at Bosco lying on the deck. "What have you got all over your coat?"

I touched his fur. He was sticky and damp, and a light coffee color where he'd normally be white.

"Is that my iced coffee you're wearing?"

"Smells like coffee to me, along with your cake," Nate said, taking a step toward us and nudging Bosco with his foot. "Up you get, mate. Looks like you need a bath, too."

"Custard slice." I sighed. I'd have to take him to the dog grooming salon, The Pooch Parlor. Unless...

At Nate's gentle nudging, Bosco clambered to his feet.

"Thanks." I dipped my head to cut off the sight of all his tempting skin and tugged Bosco to the back door of the deck.

I opened the white French door and disappeared into the sunroom. This was my favorite room in the entire house, with the wall-to-floor windows on either side of the French doors. The walls were painted a soft dove-grey, and the couch was a long, low dark grey modular. Perfect for sitting or lying on and gazing out at the beach whenever the weather was too hot or cold to sit on the deck. It had the perfect light for reading.

I lured Bosco into my bedroom and connecting bathroom and shut him in with me. If he'd go in the shower, then I wouldn't have to take him to The Pooch Parlor. I turned on the taps until the water ran warm, then shoved Bosco's rump. He dug his paws into the mat and lowered his head.

"Move," I grumbled.

My futile attempts at pushing him failed. I wrapped my arms around his solid body and lifted, but I didn't get more than his front paws off the floor by a few inches.

"How heavy are you?" I let go, releasing a puff of hot air to blow the hair off my face.

We stared at each other for a solid minute. The steady stream of water and the rising steam ticking away the time.

"Fine." I threw up my hands. "I'll take you to see Bree. She'll be happy to bathe you, but I'm not letting you out of this bathroom while I shower so you can get sticky iced coffee through the house."

Bosco lifted his head upon hearing the name, Bree. What did she have that I didn't for washing him? A bit of soap and water should be all it takes.

"Spoilt dog," I mumbled and stripped off my now dog hair and iced coffee-stained clothes, along with splatters of custard and icing sugar. I should run out and put them in the washing machine with Nate's T-shirt. Then his top might be clean before he left, and he wouldn't need to come back for it if I didn't hire him.

I creaked open the bathroom door. The hinges needed oiling. The interior might need a bit of work. Nothing I couldn't handle, though. I shut Bosco in the bathroom and hurried out of my bedroom. My bare feet raced across the kitchen to the adjoining laundry room. I threw the clothes in the washing machine after a quick sniff of Nate's T-shirt. What deodorant did he use? My husband never smelled that good.

Shaking my head at myself, I slammed the lid shut and left the laundry room. A shadow passed across the kitchen window overlooking the deck. *Shit.* I stared out the window. Nate stood on the other side. Thank goodness his back was to me. I scuttled out of the kitchen in my underwear before Nate turned around.

What a disaster of a morning.

When I opened the bathroom door, I found Bosco sound asleep, curled up on the bathmat. Great, something else I'd need to wash. I stepped under the running water and washed the stickiness from my face and hair. Yikes, I must have looked a fright, and I'd ogled the poor man as though he was a tasty pastry I wanted to bite. With any luck, he didn't notice.

I dried and dressed in a hurry, so I didn't keep Nate waiting if he'd finished with his quote already. Bosco snored softly, so I left him in the bathroom with a bowl of water and opened the window for fresh air to waft into the room.

Hurrying outside, the deck creaked under my footfalls as it usually did. Nate poked his head up from the three-foot drop to the sand at the end of the deck.

"Stop right there," he called out.

I stopped walking. "What?"

"Back up real slow and go inside. This deck isn't safe."

I so didn't need anything else bad to happen to me today. Imagine if I fell through the deck. I tiptoed backward with slow, careful steps, wondering if each step would see me falling through the deck.

"I'll come to the front door," Nate said.

"Okay," I called from the safety of the house.

My heart beat a million miles an hour. What if I'd fallen through the deck? What if Nate had fallen and sued me? I shuddered. The catastrophe would finish my bed-and-breakfast before it even started at this rate.

A knock struck the front door, and I hurried through the house to answer it.

Nate's gaze raked over my tank top and shorts, while mine noted he now wore a tank top himself. At least he'd covered most of his bronzed skin and I wouldn't be a blubbering idiot again.

He cleared his throat. "So, I've had a good look around the outside."

"Come in, Nate."

"Thanks." He smiled and stepped inside.

I closed the door and led the way into the lounge room at the front of the house. Nate sat on the navy and white floral chaise lounge while I perched on the edge of the matching club chair.

He scanned the room. "This is nice, and as you said, the interior looks in better upkeep than the exterior, but after checking the deck and finding the timber almost rotten through in sections, I'd suggest a good look at the inside, too."

I sighed. "The deck needs replacing as well as the guardrail?"

"I'm afraid so." He scratched his beard and opened his small, hand-sized notepad.

"Sounds like a big job, and a long one." Would I ever get this place opened? Summer was almost over, and I'd missed the peak tourist season.

"About three weeks for the deck, then it'll need a sealant, so more like four. I recommend using a marine-penetrating wood sealer. It'll provide long-lasting protection against moisture damage and mold growth."

My shoulders slumped. The repairs would take us into the start of autumn and the end of the peak tourist season. It didn't look like I'd be opening soon.

"And the paint?"

"A big job, too. I need to wash the surface to remove the salt and mildew first, and I'll have to paint no more than an hour after washing, otherwise, the salt adheres to the surfaces again and the paint won't stick. I'll sand between each coat, so you get a longer-lasting finish. Then I'll only need to come back every couple of years for a wash, sand, and touch-up instead of a whole redo again. You won't get any peeling or blistering this way. In the long run, it'll save you money doing it right. The premium acrylic latex paints last for five years before they need a touch-up."

"How long will it take?"

He shrugged. "Hard to say. It will depend on the weather. A week if the weather is good."

"Oh, good." I smiled, glad one thing wouldn't take long. "I assumed you were going to say longer."

"The deck is the biggest job, and the priority for the safety issues."

"I didn't realize the timber was so weak."

"Most people don't until the boards give way. Luckily, I caught you. Where is the dog?" He scanned the room.

"He's asleep in the bathroom, so I left him."

"Did you get him cleaned?"

"No." I shook my head. "He wouldn't go near the shower. I'll have to take him to The Pooch Parlor."

Nate chuckled. "The what?"

"The local dog parlor. Hope Bay is dog obsessed. The people here run many dog-related events. I'm considering making the bed-and-breakfast a dog-friendly one."

"Sounds like a good idea." He smiled, causing the crinkles at the corner of his eyes to deepen. "I'm from the next town over, Paradise Point."

I could gaze at his smiling lines all day. He didn't live far away. Which would be good if I hired him. Should I hire him when dare I admit it, I was attracted to him?

"Do you have a quote?"

"I'll write one up when I get back to the office, and I'll email you the quote tonight."

"That'll be fine." Why didn't everything just fall into place, and I could open my new business?

A muffled bark echoed against the tiled walls of the bathroom.

"That's my cue." I stood and held out my hand. "Thank you for your time, Nate. I look forward to receiving your quote."

He wrapped his warm, calloused fingers around my hand. Another jolt of awareness traveled the length of my arm. He held on longer than normal and the sensation traveled to the back of my head, tingling my scalp until my hair felt like it was alive.

"My pleasure, Madeline," he said in his deep baritone.

So much warmth came from his words that my skin vibrated with the electricity of his voice. We gazed into each other's eyes. The awareness of attraction was a tangible pull between our gazes. We each inhaled in sync. Time suspended with his hand on mine.

Bosco barked.

Time snapped back to reality. Nate's eyebrows rose as though our connection surprised him, too. He released my hand, sliding his fingers away until the tips brushed the ends of mine, as though he didn't want to stop touching me. I walked him to the front door without a word, for I couldn't talk.

What just happened between us?

Chapter Three

I swung open the door to The Pooch Parlor. The little bell above tinkled and announced our arrival. Bosco trotted inside, prancing and wagging his tail. He sure did like it here. The luminous fluorescent lights shone over the brightness of the stainless-steel countertop. The sleek industrial lines of the parlor added to the impression of its cleanliness, along with the scent of sweet-smelling shampoo. At least Bosco wouldn't reek like coffee after this.

Bree smiled in greeting. She was always happy, and more so now she'd found love. Like my daughter Katie, who'd found love in Hope Bay. I was happy for them both. There must be a love-inducing aroma in the sea breeze here. It explained the many happy couples who wandered around town hand in hand.

"Hi, Madeline. What did Bosco do this time?" Bree asked.

Alley, her assistant, stuck her head out of a room. "Is Bosco here?"

"Yes," Bree hollered.

Alley rushed from the room, her strawberry-blonde ponytail swinging. "What time did I have?"

Bree scanned a piece of paper on the counter. "Four fifteen."

"Poop." Alley sulked. "Guess I didn't win. Who did?"

"Win what?" I frowned in confusion.

Bree peered up, seeming to have forgotten I was even there. "Ah, we all bet on what time you'd bring in Bosco."

"What?"

Bree held up her hands. "It was Katie's idea. They've got one at the vet clinic too."

"Guess we're the winners, or did you take him to the vet first?"

"Katie is in so much trouble when she gets home." I tapped my foot. Wait until she came home from her supposed planned weekend away. That cheeky so-and-so. "No, I didn't take Bosco to the vet first. He spilled iced coffee on himself if you must know. Nothing too exciting."

I wouldn't tell them about the custard slice, or the broken guardrail, or the man rescuing me, the gorgeous man, who I would most likely hire to fix my house. Who knows what else they'd bet on?

"It was only fun. We didn't mean any harm by it," Alley gushed.

I relaxed. "I know, I was making you sweat. So, who won?"

Alley giggled. "That was mean, Mrs. Edwards."

"Call me Madeline. I'm soon-to-be ex, Mrs. Edwards."

Bree ran her finger down the list. "Joel had the closest time at eleven."

"Joel was in on it too?" I shook my head. "Did you all assume I couldn't look after a dog?"

"No, it's not that," Alley squeaked. "We know what Bosco's like. He's always being led by his nose, and it always leads him to trouble."

Bree rounded the counter in her trademark striking boots. "It's nothing against you. You should see how many times Hannah brings him in for me to wash."

"Really?" I raised my eyebrows.

"Between us, he's the most washed dog in Hope Bay."

I laughed. "Now you're just making me feel better."

She smiled and took Bosco's leash. Then she knelt and ruffled his head. He gazed at Bree with an adoring look. Bree slid a treat from her pocket and fed it to Bosco. So, that's her trick. Treats. I'd head over to the shops and pick up a bag of treats, then Bosco might follow me around with the same adoring expression on his face.

"He'll be ready in an hour."

"Thanks, Bree."

I left Bree's shop and stepped onto the sidewalk. The summer sun glared hotly on my head and bounced off the pavement. I strolled along the path to the supermarket and found the dog food aisle. Not one I'd usually walk along. Why were there so many products for dogs? Pet milk. Tin food. Bags of biscuits. Toys. And treats, exactly what I was searching for. There were biscuit treats, liver treats, and strips of treats. Those appeared the most appetizing. I picked up a bag and headed to the checkout.

"Good morning," the sales assistant said.

I read his name tag. "Good morning, Oliver."

"Is that all for today?" He scanned the item.

"Yes, thank you." I swiped my credit card.

"Would you like a bag?"

"No, thank you." I picked up the dog treats.

"Have a good day."

"You too."

He smiled. There was a familiarity with his smile. I paused for a second. Where had I seen him? Shrugging, I left the shop. Many people visited Hope Bay during the summer. No wonder I couldn't figure out where I'd seen him before.

My stomach rumbled. I checked my watch. Close enough to lunchtime, and I'd missed eating my custard slice. I'd head to Blissful Bites to buy another slice to eat after lunch. My mouth watered. And an iced coffee.

I shoved the dog treats into my back pocket and walked the long way to the best café in town along the esplanade and the more extravagant beachfront houses in the town. I gazed at their decks with longing. Wait a minute. If I needed to replace the deck, I should put in one more extravagant. Nothing like these, but something special for my soon-to-be guests.

Continuing on my way, I whipped out my phone and dialed the phone number for Hudson Construction.

Nate answered on the second ring. "Hudson Construction, how may I help you?"

His electrifying voice sent a shiver down my spine. I pushed my reaction aside and answered, "Nate, hi, it's Madeline Edwards. You came to my house to give me a quote this morning."

"Madeline. How could I forget you?" he asked with a hint of teasing humor.

And dare I think it, flirting?

I'd never live this morning down. At least Nate was the only one who witnessed the incident.

"I wonder if you might do a quote for a different deck?"

"A different deck? What did you have in mind?" His voice turned to business.

Business Nate I could deal with, the semi-flirty one left me flustered. He wasn't flirting, was he? It was my imagination. Surely?

"I'm not certain." Why did I call him without thinking it through? I bit my lip and said, "I figured if I need to replace the deck, why not make it better?"

"True," he said. "I'm having lunch then I can come back, or you can join me since you're heading my way."

"I am?" I swung my head to the left and right.

"Straight in front of you."

Straight in front of me was Blissful Bites. Nate sat at an outside table, phone to his ear and a smile in place. Why did he always smile?

I lifted a hand and waved. He waved back and hung up his phone. I followed suit and walked the last dozen steps toward Nate. Did he have to watch my every step? My legs wobbled like a newborn foal.

"Hi," I squawked. Was I a seagull again?

"Please join me." He waved a hand at the empty metal chair.

"I'll grab a salad and be right back."

I hurried into the café before my wobbly legs gave way. Why was the man more scrumptious looking than the custard slice?

"Hi, what can I get you?" Bailey asked.

"Can I have a salad and an iced coffee, please?"

"Have here or to go?"

"Have here."

Bailey stepped away from the counter to fetch my order. I peeked outside and unabashedly checked out Nate while his back faced me. Why did he send butterflies dancing around in my stomach? It made little sense. I was a middle-aged woman. About to get divorced. With a grown daughter, for goodness' sake.

The midday crowd filed into the café. I didn't blame them. The tasty pastries were Bailey's specialty, and I wanted my missed custard slice even more now the scent of fresh baked goods filled the place. I couldn't eat one now with the ridiculous fluttering in my stomach. A salad would be hard enough to swallow.

"Here you go, Madeline."

I spun back around in a hurry. Did she see me checking out Nate? Not that she'd know him. Would she? He was here in her café. What if she knew him and told him I'd gazed at him with longing? Because that's what I'd been doing.

Don't blush.

"Thanks," I said way too brightly.

I swiped my credit card and grabbed my purchases. For a split second, I considered sitting at another table. Don't be ridiculous. I can do this.

Smiling at Nate, I placed my salad bowl and a glass of iced coffee on the table.

"No replacement custard slice?"

"No." I sat in the chair opposite him. "One custard slice disaster in a day is all I can handle."

He chuckled, causing the smile lines to broaden around his eyes, and waved at his empty plate. "I couldn't resist eating one after smelling the sweet custard on you earlier."

I dug into the salad before the butterflies in my stomach burst through the skin.

"What do you have in mind for the new deck?"

"I'm not certain. I had a sudden idea when walking here. Have you seen the decks on the esplanade?"

"I have. If you want a deck like those, you'll need to apply for a new council permit."

"I don't want an enormous deck. I like the size and everything about the deck. Can you make it more inviting to sit and enjoy the view?"

"Hmm." He tapped his fingers on the tabletop. "Let me think."

I crunched my way through the salad and avoided looking at Nate or attempting to keep my eyes away from the man. It was hard with him sitting in front of me. All gorgeous man that he was.

"Have you checked me out?"

"What?" I spluttered with my mouth full.

A piece of carrot flew out of my mouth and hit the side of his coffee mug. Shit. My face flamed. Beetroot, here I am.

"I'm so sorry." I wiped his mug with my napkin, then wiped my mouth. He must think I'm a total food klutz. First, the custard slice in my face. Now, I spat the carrot across the table. This day was a disaster with food. Or I was the disaster.

Middle-aged woman, soon to get divorced, lusting after a man younger and hotter than her.

Idiot.

"All good. I'd finished my coffee, anyway."

"Oh, thank goodness." I sagged in the chair.

"So, have you?"

"What?" I shoved the remaining salad to the side. I wouldn't risk eating in front of Nate again.

"Checked out my website?"

"Oh." I tugged on the collar of my tank top. Of course, he didn't mean had I checked him out. "Yes, I've explored your website. You do beautiful work, and the reason I requested a quote."

He tapped away on his phone. "What about a deck like this?"

I leaned across the table to look at the image on his phone. "Nice, but not quite right."

"Yeah, I think you're right." He lifted his brilliant green eyes from the phone. Except they never met my face. He swallowed. His Adam's apple bobbed. "Ah..."

While leaning across the table, I'd inadvertently flashed him my cleavage. I sat back in the chair and picked up my iced coffee. Resisting the urge to get embarrassed yet again around Nate, I gulped the cool liquid to stave off the way my body tingled from his heated look.

He reached for his coffee cup forgetting he'd finished it. The smile lines around his eyes vanished. He shoved the cup aside, then cleared his throat. "I can design a deck for you, but as you don't know what you want, it'll make it hard."

"Yes." I tucked my hair behind my ears.

Stop it. Don't flirt with the man. I untucked my hair.

"Can you give me any ideas?"

"I want the deck to be warm and inviting. A place to snuggle and enjoy the ocean."

"How about you pop out to my office, and we can run through design ideas on the computer together?"

"Now?"

"Yeah, I have the rest of the day free. You're in luck today. The client's finances for my next job fell through. If you contract me for the job, I can start tomorrow."

"Well, Nate, let's do this. If you come up with a design, the job's yours."

He smiled. I was fast becoming attached to his smiles. They shone with such happiness. He slid his business card across the table.

"Here's my address. I'm heading to the office now, so come when you're ready."

"I'll get my car, oh, no..."

"What?"

"I have to look after Bosco."

"Bring him with you. I have a decent-sized dog-proof backyard he can stay in, and I have a dog he might enjoy the company of."

I dipped my head. Guess I'd spend even more time with the gorgeous man today after he'd rescued me, and after I'd spat food at him.

How else will I embarrass myself in his presence?

Chapter Four

I drove my little gold sedan around the last bend of Paradise Point with the music blaring. The twisting bends and curves made my stomach surge, or maybe it was the butterflies at the notion of seeing Nate again. Either way, I couldn't wait to get out of the car. I turned into the driveway of a single-story beach house painted a hazy silver-green. Was this the right place? Was this Nate's office? I checked the address on the card, then climbed out of the car and opened the back door, ready to make a lunge for Bosco's leash.

Except he didn't jump out in excitement as I'd expected.

I stuck my head in the back door. "Bosco?"

He lifted his head slowly from the back seat. His floppy ears hung lower than usual, and his eyes appeared dull.

"Are you car sick too?" I leaned inside the car and tugged his leash. "Come on, fresh air will help."

Bosco dragged himself out of the car and sniffed the ground. I sighed in relief he was back to his normal self. If I needed to take him to the vet, then I'd never live it down.

A navy-blue sign with yellow writing "Hudson Construction" hung on a solid timber gate next to the beach house and underneath sat an intercom system. I walked over with Bosco and pressed the button.

"Hello?" Nate's voice buzzed through the system.

"Hi, Nate, it's Madeline."

"Come on through." A buzzer beeped, and the gate popped open.

I shoved the wooden slats inward. Bosco raced through the gate. His nose worked with a loud snuffle and snort while his tail wagged.

A white stone path led down the side of the house and crunched under my feet. It led us into the backyard where a matching silver-green timber studio room sat separately from the house. Nate slid open the sliding glass door to the studio and stepped out.

"Did you find the place all right?"

"No problem." I surveyed the well-maintained yard. It had a lush green lawn, a row of yellow flowering shrubs, and a huge sandpit. Did Nate have small children? I didn't detect a wedding band, but a construction worker might not wear a ring.

"You can let Bosco off the leash if you like. He won't get out of the yard."

"Are you sure?"

"One hundred percent. I have a Koolie and he's a bigger escape artist than a beagle could ever be."

"What's a Koolie, and where is he?" I glanced around the yard.

"He's a working dog. I got him from my friend, Shawn, who's a dog trainer when his former owner couldn't handle him anymore."

"That was nice of you."

"He's inside the office." Nate pointed at the door he'd stepped out of. "We can keep them separate if you like."

"Good idea. I don't know how Bosco is with other dogs." I bent and patted Bosco's head then unclipped his leash. My nerves skyrocketed. If he got out, I'd likely never find him, and Hannah would be so upset.

"Trust me, he can't get out."

Was I that transparent?

I joined Nate outside his office, and he slid open the door for me. On the other side of the room, sat a large window overlooking the magnificent view from atop the hill and encompassing the beach of Paradise Point.

"What a view. Mine is good, but this beats it." I stepped up to the window and peered at the long drop over the side of the hill. Dark grey rocks, boulders, vegetation, and small, white flowers decorated the descent to the pale gold sand below.

"It's pretty good."

I spun around. Nate's smile greeted me. His gaze was intent on my face. A dog of grey, black, and white spotted patterns walked up to Nate's side. He rubbed the dog's ears affectionately. The dog watched me with his intense ice-blue eyes.

"This is Sampson. He's deaf."

"He's beautiful." I'd never seen a dog like him before. His coat was an unusual pattern of spotted colors, and his legs were fluffy with fur.

"I think so too." Another of his smiles lit Nate's face. "Come sit at the computer with me and we'll see what we can come up with for your deck."

"Okay."

Sampson followed Nate and dropped to the ground at his feet. I perched in the chair next to Nate. He clicked away on the design studio expertly. He was so close I found it hard to focus on the screen. His aftershave was even more alluring this close to him. My nose twitched on every inhale. In no time at all, Nate put the measurements of my deck into the system.

"We can't change the height or the width unless you want to apply for council permission, and they can take weeks to come back."

"No. Keep the deck the same in measurements, but what else can you add to make it more appealing?"

His hand worked fast on the mouse, and images flicked up on the screen. "What about this?"

I frowned. "No, not cozy enough."

He restarted the image. A click here, a click there. An image took shape. I leaned forward. My arm touched Nate's. Electricity ran the length of my arm. The hairs on my body stood on end at attention for another touch from Nate.

"Yes, that's it," I exclaimed.

It was like he'd picked the image from my brain. The one I couldn't explain for the life of me.

Another few clicks and Nate sat back, placed his hands on his head, and grinned.

"Perfect." I twisted toward him. My knee scraped against his. The friction was delicious.

His gaze roamed my face. "I think so too."

I tucked my hair behind my ear. He was talking about the plan, wasn't he?

"I can get cushions made for the bench seats."

"I can make them hinged so you can store the cushions underneath."

"Perfect," I said again. "I love it, Nate. You're hired."

He laughed. "Don't you want a price first?"

I laughed at myself. How eager was I?

"Right. Yes, I do. How much?"

He minimized the image and opened another program. Before my astonished eyes, numbers whirled across the screen. At the bottom sat a number. A large number. Larger than I'd considered, but doable. There's always wiggle room in business.

"Hmm." I pretended to hesitate. "Can you go lower?"

"You drive a hard bargain, Madeline." He tapped the keys again. "This is the lowest I can go."

"Deal." I held out my hand.

Nate clasped my hand and shook. Every nerve ending in my body focused on the warmth of his palm, the roughness of his fingers against my skin. I shifted closer to Nate, drawn to the sensation of his touch, the smile in his eyes, and the allure of his aroma.

Bosco barked and scratched at the door. Saved from making a proverbial fool of myself by a dog. I drew my hand out of Nate's grasp.

He rose from his chair and walked to the sliding door. Bosco raced inside and headed straight to me. He placed his front paws on my legs and covered me with sand.

"What have you been up to?" I brushed at the sand, but the grains were everywhere.

Bosco paused his exuberance over my lap and barked at the dog lying beside the chair. Sampson didn't shift. Poor thing being deaf. The reality of his handicap hit me. He wouldn't hear his name when called. He wouldn't hear other dogs greeting him, and he wouldn't hear if he were in danger.

Nate dropped back into the chair beside me and touched Sampson on his shoulder. His dog lifted his head and sighted Bosco for the first time. In an instant, he jumped to his feet and wagged his tail.

The pair of dogs touched noses. Their tails wagged happily.

"I'd say they like each other," I said.

Next, they sniffed each other's rear ends.

"I'd say so too now they've got the formal dog greeting out of the way. Shall we let them outside to play?"

"For sure. Then I can skip one of his three walks today."

"He has three walks?"

"Hannah insists he needs them."

"What he needs is dog obedience training and an outlet for his instincts." He stood and opened the sliding door.

The dogs bounded outside. I joined Nate at the door. The dogs ran laps around the yard. I chuckled at their antics.

"He needs something, that's for sure."

"I take Sampson to a friend's sheep farm and let him herd sheep. It's what he's bred for. Beagles are scent hounds. Is there somewhere he can put his nose to use?"

"Good idea. I'll mention it to Hannah."

"Would you like a drink?"

"Sure, it looks like they'll amuse each other for a while. If you're not busy, that is?"

"I'm not busy." He walked to the bar fridge in the office. "Beer, wine, soft drink, orange juice, or water?"

"Water is fine." I shifted closer. "Oh, you have my favorite wine."

"Wine then?" He grasped a miniature bottle of pink Moscato.

"I shouldn't. I have to drive back to Hope Bay."

"Another time then."

Since when did he consider we'd drink wine together? He was now my employee, and I was his boss so that wouldn't happen. It couldn't. It'd make me as bad as Garry. I should grab Bosco and head home. Nate handed me a bottle of water. I smiled my thanks. A few more minutes wouldn't hurt. Would it?

"When can you start work?"

"I'll be there first thing in the morning to tear up the old deck. I'm afraid you won't be able to use your back door until it's finished."

"That's okay, I can use the front door. I sure will miss sitting on the deck though."

"How long have you lived there?" Nate opened a bottle of beer and drank.

My gaze zeroed in on his tattooed bicep bulging while he drank. What was the pattern? It would need an up close and personal inspection, or for me to ask, and it was way too personal for an employee and employer. Wasn't it?

"A few months. How long have you lived here?"

"Eighteen years."

"Wow? I didn't think..."

"You didn't think what?"

"I didn't think you'd be old enough."

He laughed. "I'm plenty old enough."

Well, he didn't tell me how old. His eyes sparkled in amusement, as he drank his beer while looking at me. I turned to the dogs still running laps around the yard and taking turns in who chased who.

"Do you mind if I bring Sampson to work with me?"

"No, of course not."

"Thanks. He's like Bosco and needs a lot of attention."

"My daughter never needed as much attention as Hannah's dog."

"How old is your daughter?"

"Katie's twenty-two."

"Now it's my turn to say I didn't think you'd be old enough."

"I'm plenty old enough." I threw his words back. If he didn't tell me his age, I wouldn't tell him mine either.

"My son's eighteen." The smile lines around his eyes disappeared and a slight pucker twitched at his brow.

It was the first frown I'd seen on his face. Why was he frowning about his son?

"I remember eighteen. It was a hard year to parent. I bet your wife and you are finding it hard too."

"I'm not married, but his mother and I are finding the teenage years hard. You want your kids to figure things out faster than you did and not make the same mistakes, but they're like carbon copies, and he seems to be heading down the same path."

"Oh." I drank the water to get my thoughts in order. What mistakes did he make? Why wasn't he married? From where I stood, his life appeared in order with a successful business, a splendid home, and a kid he loved with the amount of worry he'd voiced for his son. "I'm sure he'll work it out."

"I hope so. At least he didn't knock up his girlfriend at sixteen. I suppose he beat me there."

I choked on the water and gasped for air through my burning throat.

"Sorry, too much over-share?"

"I'm good," I rasped and wiped my mouth.

My mind raced. Sixteen plus eighteen. Makes him thirty-four and eight years younger than me. Too young. Not that it mattered. As much as I liked Nate, as much as I was attracted to him, and as much as his touch sent jolts of electricity through my body—he wouldn't be anything more than the contractor working on my house.

Still, a woman could look.

Nate disappeared back inside his office. I exhaled. Bosco and Sampson stopped their mad running and lay on the green lawn panting. Nate returned with Bosco's leash and handed it to me.

"I'll finish the official quote and email it to you tonight."

"Thanks, Nate." I should shake his hand again, but every time I did, time stood still like we were in a cocoon of awareness.

A few weeks of watching Nate work on my house would be the definition of pleasant torture.

Chapter Five

The damp sand was cool beneath my bare feet on our morning walk. Bosco trotted in front of me on the long length of his leash, chasing the waves as they lapped at the white sand. It was like being at the beach with Katie as a toddler. So mischievous and full of fun.

How things had changed since then.

I no longer visited the beach. I lived here now. Alone. The fact was never more apparent until last night when the reality Katie wasn't in the house hit me with a heaviness that lapped on loneliness. Then Bosco jumped onto the couch and spilled my cup of tea of course, but when he'd snuggled into my side and laid his head in my lap, I couldn't resist his big, brown eyes.

When Katie moved out, I might get a dog for myself. Or a cat. They'd be less trouble than Bosco.

Bosco yanked on the leash in the opposite direction from the waves. I turned from the serenity of the water and the appeal of the surfers looking so free on their boards. What had caught Bosco's attention? A man walked along the beach, a dog at heel by his leg. If only Bosco walked like his dog.

Wait, I recognized the dog and the gorgeous man heading my way.

"Seems we had the same idea this morning," Nate said, joining me.

"It's a beautiful morning for a walk."

Nate smiled and ran his gaze over my face. "It is now."

I lifted a hand to my windswept hair. "Yes, the clouds have passed over." There was no way he meant me. Not when he looked like an Adonis.

"Shall we?" He pointed to the length of the glistening white sand.

Doubt barreled to the surface. I shouldn't walk with him. Should I? It wasn't the right thing to do, but he hadn't started working for me. Oh, why not?

"Yes, Bosco would love that."

The two dogs were happily sniffing each other in greeting by our feet.

"As would Sampson."

The butterflies fluttered again. Were we talking about the dogs or ourselves?

"Let's go, Bosco." I tugged his leash.

Nate touched Sampson on the shoulder to get his attention. The dog turned his way and fell into step with another hand signal.

"Did you teach him the hand signals?"

"Yeah, he's the same as other dogs, he just can't hear."

"I noticed you touch him in the same place to get his attention."

"It was the first thing I worked on with him. When he first came home with me, he'd startle to touch. I did a lot of research and learned to desensitize him to touch by always using the same location first and offering a food reward."

Bosco yanked on the leash in front of me, while Sampson stayed next to Nate.

"How do you do that?"

"What?"

"Keep him next to you. Bosco tugs so hard it seems like he's about to rip my arm out of the socket."

Nate chuckled. "Patience and training. Would you like to swap?"

"Will Sampson let me walk him?" I queried. I didn't want to do anything to upset Sampson.

"If you stay by my side, he'll be fine."

"Okay."

We stopped and switched leads. Bosco grew excited and ran around me.

"Stop it," I scolded and stepped over the long leash he'd wound around my ankles.

My foot caught on the leash. I teetered on one leg.

"Ah," I squawked and fell into Nate, smacking my face into his firm chest.

He wrapped his free arm around my waist and kept me upright on my one leg, while I buried my nose into his T-shirt and inhaled his intoxicating aroma. Purely accidental, of course. I couldn't stop myself from breathing. That didn't mean I didn't enjoy it.

Yet again, Nate had rescued me.

I eased myself out of his arms.

"Sorry."

Don't blush.

Nate extracted Bosco's leash from my hands and passed me Sampson's leash, who'd sat patiently by Nate's side through the whole incident.

"How long do you have Bosco?" His smile lines disappeared.

"Until tomorrow."

"Let's hope he doesn't do you grievous bodily harm before then."

I giggled. Seriously? I giggled. What was wrong with me? A grown woman giggling?

"I'm sure I'll make it to lunchtime tomorrow," I said, crossing my fingers behind my back and wishing I'd taken Katie's route and said I was unavailable to dog-sit Bosco. Now I understood her desperation to not dog-sit him again.

"Is your ankle okay?" He scanned my legs.

"It's fine. I'm fine. Let's walk."

We set off along the white sand. Sampson fell into step with Nate, not realizing I held the leash. I stuck close to Nate's side so as not to confuse the dog. Bosco, who was on the other side of Nate, jerked on his leash.

Nate tugged. "Heel."

Bosco jerked again and attempted to get in front of Nate.

"Heel." Nate tugged the leash again.

And like that, Bosco fell into step with Nate. My mouth dropped open. Of all the easiest, simplest things to do, and it worked. Ridiculous, I hadn't contemplated it.

"I received the quote last night. Thank you."

"My pleasure. I'm looking forward to giving you what you want."

I swallowed. Nate's words were so deep and husky. I wanted the new deck, but I also wanted to explore the attraction between us. It was one or the other. Deck it was. Plus, I was too old for Nate. My hair was too red. I was still married. I should call Garry again and ask him why he was taking so long to sign the joint application divorce papers.

He had a shiny young girlfriend. It wasn't like he wanted me anymore. I had my doubts he wanted me in the first place, but what was done, was done. No point dwelling on the last twenty-two years of marriage when it was over.

"My guests will love it, and so will I."

More people arrived at the beach, and the solitude and peace of the early morning gave way to the excited tourists. We turned, Bosco and Sampson stayed by our sides, and we headed back to my house as a quiet calmness settled between the four of us. It was nice not having to talk and having someone walk by my side. Nate's presence was comforting, even with the butterflies fluttering inside my stomach and the awareness of how much I was attracted to him.

Back at the house, Bosco and Sampson lapped the bowl of water and flicked drops everywhere. I took a step back, so they didn't cover me with droplets.

"Thanks for the pleasant walk." I exchanged leashes with Nate.

"My pleasure." Nate smiled. The crinkle lines around his eyes made me smile too.

"I guess I'll leave you to dismantle the deck."

"No worries, Madeline."

"Let me know if you need anything."

"Will do." He walked over to his work truck with Sampson by his side.

After a lingering look at Nate, I opened the front door and disappeared inside the house. Bosco flopped onto his bed and closed his eyes. Guess his morning walk tired him. I was a little tired too. I picked up a book and settled on the modular sofa in the sunroom even though I needed to do a million things to prepare for opening the bed-and-breakfast.

But I couldn't concentrate on the words in front of my face. Every few lines my gaze would wander to the window and Nate ripping up planks of timber from the deck. The sun shone off his mirrored sunglasses and hid his smile lines, but I imagined he smiled while he worked. He always smiled.

He flicked his hair back from his face. My gaze followed his fingers of its own accord.

I turned back to the book. I read the same line five times. My gaze wandered back to Nate. Beads of sweat ran down his bulging biceps. The late summer morning sun must have grown hotter. I bit my lip.

Disgusted at myself, I threw the book aside and stood. Nate's head lifted in my direction. Shit, did he realize I'd been checking him out? I walked to the French door and swung it open.

"Would you like a drink?"

"I'm good, thanks." He held up a water bottle.

I dipped my head and shut the door. Then I walked into the kitchen, my second favorite room in the house. Decorated with peacock blue wall tiles, it contained glossy white cupboards and a massive island bench fitting four barstools on one side. Plus, the oversized oven would be perfect for cooking for my future guests. I needed to keep myself busy and stop watching Nate. Cooking it was. There was a familiar recipe I used to cook at the silk farm I wanted to put a twist on and make into a special lunchtime dish for the bed-and-breakfast. There was no time like the present.

I flicked on the radio and set to work while dancing around the kitchen to the songs blaring. This was more like it. I sifted the flour wriggling my hips. I spun to the song and opened the fridge. Then cracked the eggs and added the milk. Humming away to the next song, I stirred the mixture with a wooden spoon until the batter was ready.

Now for the twist.

Cracked pepper cheese, diced salami, and sweet red capsicum. Would the muffins be too spicy for the average person?

I poured the batter into a muffin tin and placed the tray in the hot oven. While waiting for the muffins to cook, I washed the dishes. The window overlooked the deck, and subsequently Nate. He'd taken off his T-shirt. Beads of glistening sweat rolled down his back and chest. My hands stopped moving. His chest had been firm under my face. What would it be like under my hands?

The timer on the oven buzzed.

Nate's head lifted.

I ducked and dropped to the floor.

Idiot. Caught staring again!

My heart pounded, and I crab-walked out of the kitchen and into the hallway, out of view of the window. Taking a deep, calming breath, I stood. I wrapped my hair into a ponytail, then walked into the kitchen. Nate was no longer looking at the kitchen window. I sighed in relief and opened the oven.

The muffins looked and smelled amazing. The warm aroma of melted cheese and baked food filled the kitchen. I tipped the muffins onto the cooling rack. Would Nate be a willing guinea pig to sample them?

I walked to the French door and opened it, but Nate wasn't in view. Disappointment settled the fluttering butterflies in my stomach as I shut the door. He must have left for the day. It was getting hot outside. Too hot to be doing manual labor.

A knock sounded on the front door. I hurried to answer it, the butterflies fluttered again hoping it was Nate. I opened the door. Nate stood there looking altogether way too gorgeous for someone who'd been working for the last few hours.

The butterflies in my stomach flared to life making every nerve in my body come alive too.

"Hope you don't mind, I'm calling it quits for the day." He put a hand on the doorframe and leaned his head inside. "What smells so delicious?"

"I made a batch of muffins," I said, tugging on my ponytail. "And I wondered if you'd mind sampling them. They're a new recipe."

"Mind? Are you kidding? If they taste as good as they smell, then I'm more than happy."

"Good." I smiled and waved him into the house.

Nate and Sampson followed the scent to the kitchen. Nate leaned over the warm muffins and inhaled.

"I can't wait to try one. Where can I wash my hands?"

"The bathroom's down the hallway on the right."

"I'll be back in a sec."

Sampson followed Nate. It was sweet how the dog always stuck to his side. Unconditional love. I sighed.

Why didn't humans love like dogs?

Chapter Six

Nate straddled one of my chrome and black barstools and swiped a muffin from the plate. He split the muffin into two parts. Steam wafted, and he inhaled before sliding a piece into his mouth. I crossed my fingers that the flavors worked.

Nate chewed, swallowed, then smiled and ate the rest in one bite.

"Well?" I twisted my wedding ring.

"Delicious." He grabbed another muffin.

"Thank goodness." I sagged against the counter. "Would you like a coffee?"

"Sure, if you're making one."

"I am." I shuffled around the kitchen, suddenly self-conscious with a man in the room. Not just any man, but one I found attractive. One who I'd employed. Would he be sitting here with me if I didn't? "How do you take it?"

"Black, one sugar," he said.

The same way I drank my coffee. I shook off the coincidence. It wasn't a sign. No. I was too old for ridiculous imaginings.

The aroma of coffee filled the air and mingled with the warm muffin scent. I placed Nate's mug on the bench and sat on the barstool next to him and blew on my coffee before taking a sip.

"Can I ask you something, Madeline?"

I exchanged my cup for a muffin. "Sure."

He picked up his mug and sipped the black coffee. Butterflies fluttered with ferocity in my stomach at what he wanted to ask.

"Why are you wearing a wedding ring if you're not together anymore?"

"Oh." I touched the wedding ring. "It's not what you're probably thinking."

"What do you suppose I'm thinking?"

"I want my husband back."

He sipped his coffee and stared at me over the rim of his mug. "Do you?"

"Heavens no." I exhaled loudly. "I wear the band still for my integrity because I made a promise when I put on the ring and said the vows and I intend to keep my promise. When Garry signs the divorce papers, I'll take off the ring and give it back to him. Not that he'd want the wedding band, but because it's the right thing for me to do."

Silence descended in the room. I picked at the muffin and put tiny pieces in my mouth. It was quite good. The flavors were spicy, but not too hot and overbearing.

Nate touched my wedding ring with his finger. "What happened?"

"Oh, the usual—a younger woman happened."

Nate scowled. "Your husband's a fool if he'd give you up for a younger woman. You have integrity, class, and a big heart."

"How do you know I have a big heart?"

"You're watching your sister's dog, who is the most problematic dog I've ever seen, and only someone with a big heart would do that."

I laughed. Bosco was curled up in his bed, sleeping the afternoon away.

"Bosco's not all bad."

Nate smiled. "Besides." He leaned closer to me, his lips within kissing distance. "A younger woman has nothing you don't have."

The muffin fell out of my fingers and bounced off the counter onto the floor. "What?"

"You're beautiful with a smoking hot body, surely you know that?"

"Um, Nate." I slid off the stool and picked up the muffin. Did he think that about me? Why did his words make me glow with happiness? But... "This isn't appropriate since, you know, I hired you to fix my deck."

"Most definitely not." He stood too. "I'm sorry. I won't be inappropriate again."

"Good." I dipped my head. It's what I want, isn't it?

We stared at each other. Inappropriate imaginings jumped into my head. Of him and me doing very inappropriate things. I blinked. He should go, shouldn't he? I should ask him to leave, shouldn't I? I shouldn't have let him inside the house, but I did.

"Do you have a tape measure?" I asked instead.

"In the truck. What do you want me to measure?"

"The bedroom windows upstairs, if you have time. I'd like to order new curtains."

"Not a problem. I'll be back."

Nate walked out of the kitchen with Sampson at his heels. Bosco lifted his head from his bed and gave them a curious glance, then rolled over and went back to sleep. I let go of the breath in my lungs and sagged onto the stool.

I was in way over my head. When was the last time a man flirted with me? Nate was flirting, wasn't he? Oh, shit, maybe he wasn't, and I was an idiot, but he called me beautiful with a smoking hot body. If he wasn't flirting, what was it?

The front door opened, and I jumped up from the stool. What was I thinking? Now I'd asked him to go into multiple bedrooms with me. I should smack my head against the counter. Maybe I'd knock sense into myself.

"Ready." He held up the tape measure.

"Yes." I forced myself out of the kitchen and up the stairs. My heart pounded a million beats a minute. I opened the first bedroom door.

Nate walked past me and flicked open the tape measure. He measured the width and height of the window, then withdrew a notepad and wrote the measurements. I didn't even remember a notepad. I must look like a complete idiot.

"Next," Nate said.

I left the room with Nate breathing down my back. Literally. He was so close, his warm breath blew on the nape of my neck with my hair tied up in a ponytail. Tingles of arousal rushed over my skin. I couldn't open the door fast enough. Nate measured the bedroom window.

I hurried out of the room. Four to go. I could do this and not imagine jumping into bed with him. Couldn't I?

It'd been way too long since...

Don't think about it.

Nate measured the next window. I stared at his cute ass encased in the denim jeans, and he'd said I had a hot body. From my point of view, he was the one with the desirable body. He wrote in the notepad and turned. My gaze landed on his crotch.

Somebody save me now from humiliating myself further.

Nate walked toward me, and I flicked my gaze to his face. He grinned. I gulped and fled the room.

Two bedrooms to go. One was the honeymoon suite.

I opened the next door and stood outside with my back to Nate. No way would I let him catch me ogling him again. How many times had he caught me now? Too many for a middle-aged woman, but around Nate, I didn't feel old.

He pressed a hand to my shoulder, and I jumped from the way my body responded to his.

"Sorry," he said. "You seemed a million miles away."

"Ah, yeah." I hurried along the hallway to the door at the end.

"After you," Nate said, holding the door.

I slipped inside the room, for the first time seeing the setting through the eyes of someone who envisioned sex. I pressed a hand to my cheek. Was I blushing? I was so hot and flustered. I didn't think I'd blushed though.

"This is very romantic," Nate said, walking by the bed.

"It's the honeymoon room." I waved a hand at the scarlet cushions on the bed. "Hence the splash of red."

"Nice touch. What color curtains will you pick?"

"I'm not sure. I like the clean lines of the white linens, but I love the seduction of the red."

Nate measured the window and jotted in his notepad. He walked over to me standing by the bed.

"I like red. It screams of seduction." His gaze landed on my hair. "What about your bedroom?"

Red. My hair's brick red. Seduction. My bedroom?

"Wh...at?"

"Do you want me to measure your bedroom window?"

"Oh." My eyes widened. "No. No, thank you. These are all the windows I need to be measured."

"Right." He ripped a few pieces of paper from his notebook and held them out.

I reached for them, and our fingers touched sending a spark of electricity between us.

"Thanks for your help."

"My pleasure." His gaze dropped to my lips.

My gaze traveled to his lips. The little bubble thing happened again, where it was him and me suspended in time. My heart pounded in my ears. The butterflies in my stomach threatened to burst free.

Loud barking echoed.

I breathed in his alluring aroma. Nate smiled. I swayed closer.

The barking drew closer. Bosco bounded into the bedroom and jumped on the bed bursting the bubble between us.

"Bosco, get down." I stepped away from Nate and the temptation of his lips and grabbed Bosco's collar to drag him from the bed.

"Yeah, he's not so bad."

"Shush," I scolded him too.

I shoved Bosco out of the bedroom and shut the door. Nate chuckled and followed me down the stairs. Sampson lay on the kitchen floor where Nate had left him and lifted his head at the sight of Nate. Nate made a hand signal and Sampson walked over to his side while Bosco yapped in excitement. He must have renewed his energy with his nap.

"I should take him for a walk."

"You can't."

I folded my arms. "Why not?"

"Because it's too hot and the pavement will burn his feet."

"Oh, right, I didn't think of that. Thanks."

"Don't worry, Madeline, you'll get the hang of looking after a dog."

"Hannah is back tomorrow. Next time she goes away, I'll say I'm busy." I laughed.

Nate laughed with me. "Wise plan." He checked his watch. "I should get going."

"Hot date?" I asked. Where did that come from?

"No such luck." He patted Sampson's head. "I'm taking my son and his mother out for dinner."

"You're together?"

"No. Our attempt at a happy family lasted two weeks after we found out she was pregnant. We realized we might have been boyfriend and girlfriend, but we'd never be more if that makes sense."

"I'm not sure." I frowned.

He rubbed a finger on his beard. "Like you, I made a promise to always be there for my son even though his mother and I didn't work as a couple. We wanted to remain friends, so we did.

I worked away a lot when he was younger, so the dinners became a thing when I was home, and we've continued them now."

"I'm impressed, Nate. Few men would take their ex out for dinner."

There's no way my ex would ask me out to dinner with our daughter. If he did, it might help repair their relationship. I hated seeing the distance growing between them, and neither seemed willing to repair it.

"I suppose not." He shrugged.

"Do you think..."

"What?"

"Never mind." I shook my head. It wasn't my place to ask. Or know.

"Ask," he urged.

What is this man doing to me? Everything I'd ever thought about myself was being blown to pieces in his presence.

"Do you think your ex wants more with you and that's why she agrees to the dinners?" The moment the words left my mouth, I regretted them. "Sorry, it's none of my business."

"I'm one hundred percent certain she doesn't," Nate said. "She's married to a great guy and their second baby is on the way."

"How do you feel about that? Shit, sorry, again."

He inched closer to me. "I'm happy for her, and me."

I tugged on my ponytail.

"It gives me hope one day I'll find someone."

With those words uttered and floating in the air between us, Nate smiled and sent the butterflies fluttering again.

I swallowed. "I'll see you tomorrow."

"Tomorrow's Sunday. I don't work Sundays. I'll see you Monday."

"Okay," I whispered.

I walked Nate and Sampson to the front door and shut it behind them before I ogled him again and he caught me, again. I wasn't myself around Nate.

But then again, maybe I was finding myself. Instead of being the dutiful wife. The one who'd never truly felt loved. We'd been content in our marriage, or I'd believed we were until I'd walked in on him with our junior assistant.

I should have been angry, but I wasn't.

It was like Garry had lifted an immense weight from my shoulders when he'd cheated. Our marriage was over. Ridiculous, I'd felt relief.

I walked into the empty kitchen, opened a bottle of wine, and gazed at the magnificent view of the ocean from the window. The deck lay in tatters underneath, but it would come back, better and more beautiful than the original.

Perhaps the same could be said for me.

Chapter Seven

Birds sang their joyous morning song chirping and tweeting in the trees and bushes of Hope Bay's nature reserve. I'd slept the best night's sleep of my life with Bosco by my side. It was funny how the presence of a dog created comfort. I bent and ruffled Bosco's ears.

"Wait." I hauled him to a stop. "Let me tie my shoelace."

Bosco sat. Since when did he obey me? I bent over before Bosco changed his mind about being good and tied my shoelace. Footsteps crunched on the gravel path behind me. I peered through my legs while bent over. I stood in a hurry and flicked my hair over my shoulders.

"Looks like I am seeing you today," Nate greeted with his trademark smile.

"Hi...um...hey." The butterflies in my stomach fluttered to life once more in his presence.

Nate stopped on the path. Sampson sat by his side, obedient as always.

"You're out early for a Sunday morning," Nate remarked.

"I'm an early riser." I shrugged. "But so are you out early, and in Hope Bay."

"I walk Sampson here every Sunday morning. It's a great walking trail."

"I didn't know you walked here."

"So, you're not stalking me then?"

My mouth fell open.

"Joking." He grinned.

My face heated. Beetroot, here I come. If I'd known Nate walked the nature trail, I would have wanted to come here too. The man enticed me to want to spend time with him. I couldn't deny my attraction to Nate. Bosco yanked on the leash and snapped me out of my stupor.

"I wanted to check out the trail for my future guests. I'm planning to make picnic baskets for lunch and send them here with a map. The reserve looks good so far. Would tourists like that?"

"No doubt. Are you making your delicious muffins for the picnic baskets?"

"I am." He made me so happy saying my muffins were delicious. "I'll add a bottle of wine, cheese, crackers, and seasonal fruit too."

He patted his firm stomach. "I'm hungry listening to you. It sounds like a perfect romantic date."

I pictured Nate and me on a picnic in the reserve with a soft blanket, a basket of goodies, and the sounds of nature serenading us. A romantic date. I shook my head and shoved my hair out of my face. Bosco whined and tugged on the leash. I ignored him.

"How was your dinner last night?"

"Same old stuff. Oliver ate like a horse but didn't talk much. Angela, his mom, nagged him about getting a full-time job. So, yeah, just one big happy family—not."

I laughed. "Thank goodness. I thought you were too perfect to be true."

"Me perfect?" He scratched his beard.

I dipped my head. He looked perfect, and he sounded perfect. He even smelled perfect.

Bosco barked, a high-pitched continuous yap.

"Stop it, Bosco," I scolded.

He tugged on the leash and dragged me a few steps toward the bushes on the side of the path. Something stirred on the ground. Brown. Long. Scaly. My heart stopped in fear. Bosco lunged forward at the movement. I stepped in front of him.

The snake struck in defense and slithered away with a speed I'd never have imagined. Bosco whined. My heart restarted with a pounding dread.

"Did the snake bite Bosco?" I trembled from head to foot.

"No." Nate scowled. "Don't move. Stay calm. Okay."

He swooped me up into his arms.

"What are you doing?" I wrapped my arms around his neck in an instinct of hanging on.

"Just stay calm." He trod along the path with long strides.

"Nate?"

"The snake bit you."

"Oh."

His fast walk turned into a jog.

"In my back pocket is my mobile phone. Pull it out and call an ambulance."

"But—"

"Do it." He ran faster to the entrance of the nature reserve.

I slid my hand into his back pocket. This was way more intimate than I imagined. I dialed emergency services and told them a snake bit me and our location. They said exactly what Nate said. Stay calm and don't walk or move and place a compression bandage on my leg if I had one.

"Do you have a bandage?" I asked Nate.

"First aid kit in the truck," he puffed.

"They said to bandage my leg."

The parking lot appeared through the trail and Nate's truck. The operator asked me if I experienced any symptoms.

"I'm okay. No, no nausea or dizziness, or headache."

Nate reached his truck and balanced me on my feet as though I was made of breakable glass, then unlocked the door and sat me in the front seat.

"Don't move." He pointed.

"I won't." The operator still talked on the phone. "Yes, I'm still here. No, no symptoms."

Nate returned and wrapped a bandage around my leg. Then he used a marker to mark a spot on the bandage. I couldn't even look at my leg. Were there bite marks? Puncture holes? The notion made me queasy.

"I might be sick," I said.

Nate unwrapped another bandage and wrapped my leg from my ankle to my thigh. Under other circumstances, I'd find his firm bronzed fingers on my thigh exciting, but right now, I was too panicked to imagine him that way.

"Relax," Nate said insistently and kept wrapping my leg. "The ambulance is on its way."

"Nate." I grabbed his shirt with both hands. "I don't want to die."

"You won't." He placed his hands over mine. "Most snake bites are dry bites."

"What the hell are dry bites?"

"When the snake bites and doesn't release its venom."

"Yeah?"

"Yes." He squeezed my hands. "Here comes the ambulance."

"Where's Bosco?" I peered over Nate's shoulder but didn't see him.

"The dogs are in the back of the truck. They're safe."

I released a breath.

"It was crazy of you to step in front of the snake."

I let go of his shirt and folded my arms. "I couldn't let the snake bite Bosco. Dogs die more than humans from snake bites, right?"

"Yes, but—"

The ambulance officers jumped out of the vehicle and rushed toward me.

"I'm fine," I assured them. Funny how I wasn't queasy anymore. It must have been the notion of puncture holes, yep, there's the queasiness in my stomach again.

They wheeled the gurney over and strapped me onto it.

"Wait! Nate?"

He rushed up to my side and took my hand. "I'm here."

"Can you take Bosco to the vet and get him checked, to be sure, please?"

"See, big heart." He squeezed my hand and let go. "I will, then I'll come and see you in the hospital."

The ambulance officers loaded me into the back of the ambulance. Thank goodness I had ambulance coverage, otherwise, this would have been an expensive morning walk. Nate's worried face peered in the back at me before the officers shut the doors.

It hit me then, I was well and truly alone.

Tears welled, but I fought them back. Nate's firm words echoed in my head: *Relax. Stay calm. I'm here.*

In the moment of uncertainty with death a real possibility, I understood one thing—I liked Nate.

Chapter Eight

The last time I'd stayed in the hospital was when I'd given birth to Katie. A long time ago. This was nowhere near as exciting as being in the maternity ward about to meet my baby.

The doctors and nurses fussed around me. They'd set up an intravenous drip and had the crash cart ready to go. I learned the toxins in a brown snake bite might cause cardiac arrest or the chance of anaphylactic shock which could be fatal. So far, I'd dodged both when they'd removed the bandages Nate had so expertly put on my leg.

The first lot of blood tests they'd drawn returned with excellent results. They'd take another lot in an hour. It was all a waiting game, and I didn't like to wait. I stared at the stark white ceiling. Alone. The beep of the monitor connected to my heart and blood pressure was the only companion besides the nurses and doctors. I should call Hannah and Katie. They'd want to know I was in the hospital, but I loathed to worry them.

I'd wait a little while longer. No point stressing my family if there was no need.

The nurse opened the door. "Your husband is here."

I grimaced. My face probably looked like I'd sucked on a lemon. What's Garry doing here? Who called him? My husband was the last person I expected or wanted to see.

Nate stepped into the room. My eyebrows rose in astonishment.

"Maddy my wife." He winked. "How are you?"

I bit my lip to stop myself from laughing, and my eyes filled with suppressed tears of laughter.

"She's doing well. No signs of envenoming." The nurse took my watery eyes for emotion.

"Good to hear." He stepped to the side of the bed and held my hand.

A buzzer rang in the corridor.

"I'll be back soon. Buzz if you experience any symptoms, a headache, or dizziness, nausea—anything," the nurse said.

I nodded my head. The door closed behind her. I burst out with suppressed laughter.

Nate's shoulders shook. "Sorry, it was the only way they'd let me in here."

"How did you explain the absence of your wedding ring?" I lifted his hand in mine.

"I'm a construction worker, and the ring gets in the way."

"Well played." I grinned.

"How are you?"

"I'm fine." My grin dropped, and I scanned the room.

"It's okay to be frightened. I'd be scared too if it were me."

I rolled my head toward Nate. "Thanks for coming."

He glanced around the sterile room. "I'd say my pleasure, but no one enjoys being in the hospital."

"The last time I was in the hospital I gave birth."

"Yeah? How old were you?"

"Twenty." I sighed remembering the happiness of the occasion. "I was so excited to meet my baby."

"Weren't you scared? Because it petrified me when Angela went into labor. I don't know what I expected, but it wasn't what happened. The birth was like a freaking horror movie with all the screaming and body fluids."

I giggled. "You were there for the birth of your son at sixteen?"

"Yeah. I guess I was excited to meet him too."

We had so much in common. Nate's hand was warm and comforting in mine. I could hold on and never let go.

"Do you want more kids?" I asked.

"Me?" He shrugged. "I don't know. They're hard work. I love my son, but, yeah, I don't know if I'd do it again. What about you?"

"At my age?" I scoffed. "No."

"You're not old, you're what? Forty-two?"

I dipped my chin. Guess I'd slipped with my age somewhere in our conversations, and I'd tried to keep my age from the gorgeous man who was way too good-looking to want anything to do with me. Why was he here holding my hand? Comforting me when all he was, was my contractor? My heart picked up speed. The beeping of the machine matched my heart.

Nate's smile lines disappeared. "Are you okay?"

"I'm fine."

"I'm calling the nurse, just in case." He stood and pressed the green call button.

"Nate, I'm fine."

"But your heart rate increased." He pointed at the screen.

"Because of you," I whispered.

"Me?"

He stared into my eyes.

I licked my lips. "You're amazing."

"Amazing?"

"Yes, you're here with me now when you don't have to be. You talk to me, really talk to me, if you know what I mean."

"You talk to me too." He squeezed my hand.

"And you are drop-dead gorgeous." My heart rate beeped faster again.

The nurse walked into the room. "What's going on in here?" She checked the readout on the machine.

"I'm fine," I told her. "Just my sexy husband here sends my heart racing." I threw Nate a shy smile.

She narrowed her eyes at me and Nate. I felt like a naughty kid.

"It's time for more blood tests. Can you leave for a few minutes, Mr. Edwards?" She gave him a pointed look.

"Not a problem, I'll grab a coffee."

Nate sauntered out of the hospital room. I laid my head back on the stiff pillows and sighed. My heart rate dropped back to its normal rate with Nate out of the room.

The nurse pursed her lips. "Guess the spike in your pulse was your husband's fault. Are you newlyweds?"

"Sort of, new." There's no way I'd tell her he wasn't my husband, and we'd only met a few days ago. Then they wouldn't allow him back into my room, and I wanted to see him again. I wanted his comforting presence to take my mind off the snake bite.

The nurse drew more blood.

"How many more blood tests?" I stared at the white ceiling instead of the blood pooling in the vial.

"Sorry, there'll be a few more blood tests before we can determine there's no envenomation and a need for antivenom."

Nate wandered back into the room.

The nurse pointed a finger at Nate. "No getting your new wife excited now. She needs to stay calm."

"Yes, nurse." He tipped his coffee cup her way.

The nurse left the room with my blood samples. Nate and I gazed at each other and snickered.

"How's Bosco?"

"See, big heart," he said. "You're worried about the dog when you're in the hospital. I dropped Bosco off at the Creature Comforts Veterinary Clinic. He didn't show any symptoms of a snake bite, but they said they'd keep him overnight for observation."

"Thanks for taking him. I guess I should call Hannah and let her know where Bosco is."

"And you," Nate said. "Does your family know you're here?"

"No." I shook my head. "I don't want them to worry."

"Maddy."

My heart rate spiked again. He gave me a nickname. Does it mean he likes me too?

"All right. Can you hand me my mobile phone please?"

Nate fetched my phone from the side table and handed it to me. "Would you like me to wait outside?"

"No, that's okay." I unlocked the screen and pulled up my contacts. Then closed the phone again. "You know what, I'll wait until the next blood test results come back."

"Fine, but you're stuck with me until your family gets here."

"I may never call them." I giggled. Seriously? I'm in the hospital with a potentially deadly snake bite and giggling with happiness.

Nate chuckled.

Four hours later, my phone rang. I jumped, absorbed in the conversation with Nate. We'd talked about anything and everything. I was sure we'd never run out of things to talk about.

I answered the call without looking. "Hello?"

"Madeline, where are you? I'm home but you're not. Are you out walking Bosco?"

"Hannah, I...ah...don't be alarmed, okay?"

"Madeline, what is it?" Her voice rose even with my warning.

"I'm in the hospital."

"What?" she screeched. "Why? Are you okay? Stupid, of course not, otherwise you wouldn't be in the hospital."

"I'm okay," I said. "A snake bit me."

"Oh my God," she gasped.

"It's okay, Hannah. I'm okay."

"But a snake bit you! I'm coming to the hospital. I'll be there soon." She hung up the phone.

"Well." I rolled my eyes at Nate "That went as well as I expected."

Nate smiled. "It's understandable she'd worry."

"I guess I should call Katie now." My finger tapped the phone for Katie's number.

"Hey, Mom," Katie said.

She sounded happy. The happiest she'd been since her dad's and my marriage breakup, and I had Joel to thank for her happiness. The man fell in love with my beautiful daughter and she fell in love with him.

"Hi, Katie." I swallowed the lump in my throat.

"We'll be home for dinner tonight."

"Um, well, here's the thing," I said. "I'm fine. There's nothing to worry about, but I'm in the hospital for observation from a snake bite."

A thump sounded. Then silence. I waited for Katie to speak.

"Hello," Joel said.

Oh, this was going so well.

"Hi, Joel, is Katie okay?"

"She dropped the phone and ran off crying. What's wrong?"

I sighed. "A snake bit me and I'm in the hospital for observation."

"Ah. What sort of snake?"

"A brown snake."

"When were you bitten?"

"This morning."

"Any symptoms?"

Trust the level-headedness of a vet to ask the appropriate questions and not go off on a worry spree like my sister and daughter.

"No. They believe it might have been a dry bite, but they're being cautious."

"Good to hear. I guess we'll see you soon. Kate is dragging our bags out to the car."

"Try to calm her down, Joel."

"I will." He hung up the phone.

Nate squeezed my hand. "Sounds like your family loves you."

"Bunch of panic merchants," I scoffed.

He chuckled. "I have to say I panicked too when the snake bit you."

"Thanks for rescuing me again."

"Careful, I might get a hero complex."

"Don't worry." I laughed. "Hannah will take Bosco home and I won't need rescuing again."

"Shame." He grinned. "I liked having an excuse to spend today with you."

Chapter Nine

Hannah burst into the hospital room, her dark russet auburn hair a disarray of soft curls. She skidded to a stop with a swish of her long emerald green dress, ran her gaze over Nate, then launched herself at me.

"Oh my God, Madeline."

I patted her back and wriggled in her embrace. "You're suffocating me."

"Sorry." Hannah let go and sat on the edge of the bed. "What happened?"

"Ah."

"She stepped between a snake and your dog, Bosco," Nate supplied.

Hannah swung her head in Nate's direction. "And you are?"

"The guy who saved your sister from your dog."

"What's that supposed to mean?" Hannah stood.

Nate folded his arms. "It means your dog is a menace and needs serious training."

"Now wait just a minute." Hannah waved her hands in the air. "Who are you?"

"All right, you two stop it," I scolded, then rolled my eyes. Anyone would think they were children with how they were behaving. "I'm fine. No reason to get worked up."

Nate tapped his fingers on his folded biceps. My gaze slid to the tattoo his fingers touched. I'd like to trace the lines of his tattoo with my finger or lips and ask him about it.

"But..." I tugged Hannah back onto the bed. "Nate's right, Bosco needs training."

Hannah threw up her hands. "I've tried, believe me. He won't do anything."

Nate unfolded his arms and released the tension from his shoulders. "One of my friends is a dog trainer. I can give you his number if you like."

"Yes, please." Hannah smiled for the first time since coming into the room. "Nate, is it?"

He stood and offered his hand. "Nate Hudson, nice to meet you."

Hannah shook his hand. "How do you know my sister?"

The nurse entered the room and scowled.

"You're such a comedian, Hannah." I pushed her shoulder. "You know Nate, my husband."

Hannah's eyes bulged. I eyeballed the nurse. Hannah's face lit with understanding.

"I'm checking the snake bite didn't affect your head," Hannah jumped to the rescue.

Nate brushed my hair back from my face. "There's nothing wrong with Maddy's head. It's beautiful."

Hannah mouthed, *Who is he?*

I ignored her and asked the nurse, "Are the last blood test results back?"

"Yes, all clear again. We won't need to do another blood test for six hours now."

"Good. I'm like a pin cushion."

The nurse's lips thinned. Could she have any less of a bedside manner? What's the harm in making a few jokes when in the hospital? It sure lightened the gravity of the situation.

"I'll stick pins in you." Hannah nudged my arm. "Then next time you won't step in front of a snake."

"But Bosco."

"I love Bosco, but you're my sister, and I love you more."

"Love you too, Freckles."

"Hey, my freckles are almost nonexistent now."

"I can see one here." I pointed to her nose. "And one here." I pointed to her forehead and tapped my finger against it.

"Knock it off, Ginga Ninja." She swatted my hand. "You should rest."

I held up my hands. Nate chuckled at our antics. Garry used to tell us to grow up when we teased each other.

"Yes, she should rest." The nurse scribbled in the chart. "You'll be staying overnight for observation."

"But I'm fine."

"We may miss subtle neurotoxicity at night. You'll be fit for discharge in the morning, all going well tonight." She left the room.

I glared at the nurse's retreating form.

"How do you two know each other?" Hannah glanced between us.

"Nate is the contractor fixing my deck."

Hannah chewed her bottom lip. "Why were you with my sister when a snake bit her?"

I rolled my eyes. "Hannah, it was pure luck."

Nate scratched his beard. "We met on the nature trail in Hope Bay walking our dogs today."

"You have a dog?"

"He has a Koolie," I said. "He's beautiful and super obedient even though he's deaf."

"Okay, I get it." She threw her hands up in the air again. "I'll get help with Bosco. Can I have the phone number please?"

"I'll give you his card tomorrow. I should get going." Nate stood.

"I'll see you tomorrow?" The thought of Nate leaving made the machines beep faster.

"Yes. I'll be working on your deck tomorrow." Nate regarded the machines. "If you need anything, don't hesitate to contact me."

"Thanks," I said softly. I didn't want him to leave. "Before you go, can you tell me one thing?"

"Sure, what's that?"

"Are there giant holes in my leg? Because the thought of two enormous holes with venom leaking out of them makes me queasy."

Nate chuckled and shook his head. "No, there are no holes. It looks like two tiny scratches on your leg."

"Oh, thank goodness." I relaxed on the pillows.

Nate squeezed my hand and smiled down at me then left. The door shut with a soft click.

"Madeline Anne Edwards, what is going on with you and your contractor? I'm gone two days and you're suddenly married to him!"

"We're not married, dingus. He only said he's my husband, so they'd let him see me in here."

"Yes, but why? If he's only your contractor working on your deck, then why was he here with you?" She folded her arms.

"I can't explain it." I twisted the edge of the blanket in my fingers. "From the moment I met him it's like this...I don't know...pull, I guess."

"And the fact he's hot has nothing to do with it?"

"You should see him without his top."

"When did you—"

The door flew open, and Katie rushed into the room.

"Mom." She hiccupped and slammed a hand over her mouth.

Hannah stood and gave Katie access to me. Katie fell into my open arms, and I hugged her tight knowing she needed a mother's comforting embrace. The hug that said I would always be here for her, and I was. I wasn't going anywhere. Even if the snake envenomed me, I would fight to live. I wasn't ready to die. Not when life had living left in it.

I wrapped my arms tighter around Katie. I wouldn't leave until I held my grandbabies, hopefully, great-grandbabies too. Lots of little redheads running around Hope Bay. I nodded my head at Joel who stood by the side of the bed. With him in the family, and I hoped he would be, his red hair would add to our side and guarantee little red-haired babies.

Katie sat back and wiped her teary eyes.

"I'm fine." I brushed her curly, fiery locks back from her worried face.

Her bottom lip trembled. "I was so scared, Mom. I don't want to lose you."

"Hey, I'm not going anywhere." I rubbed her arm. "Not yet anyway. I'll be home in the morning. The nurse said all my tests are normal, so no venom."

"You were very lucky," Joel said.

"I was, but even if the snake envenomed me, the doctors and nurses know how to treat it. How was your weekend away?"

Katie glanced at Joel. The love in their eyes was a tangible thing.

"Wonderful," she said. "And romantic."

Joel blushed. It was the most endearing trait of his.

"And the bed-and-breakfast competition stalking?"

Katie laughed. "We weren't stalking. We were checking out the competition for you."

"Same thing. What was it like?"

"It was lovely. The place was smaller than your house, the bedrooms too. The furnishings were outdated but nice. It had this homey atmosphere to it, but I'm sure you'll do better."

"Sounds like a nice place to stay."

"It was. We walked along the riverbank. Browsed the small art gallery and antique stores in Mount Cyan. It was a tiny town, and the bed-and-breakfast does well according to the owner, so having one here in Hope Bay should do even better. So many tourists come here in summer."

"Yes, I'm worried no one will come in winter though."

"I have an idea," Hannah said. "What about holding writers' retreats in the winter months?"

"I love your idea." I sat up in the bed. "It would keep the place busy all year round. You two are geniuses. I can't wait to go home and get started on writerly stuff."

"Writerly stuff?" Hannah cackled. "Lucky you have a sister who's a writer and can help you."

"I'm counting on it, Hannah. Besides, you owe me for dog-sitting Bosco."

Katie and I looked at each other and said, "Never again."

Chapter Ten

After an uncomfortable night in the hospital, I was glad to arrive home. It was funny how the beach house felt like home after I'd lived on the silk farm for so many years. I'd never expected this emotion of rightness to fill me.

"Stop fussing," I scolded Katie who'd sat me on the couch in the sunroom and draped a blanket over my lap.

"But you just got out of the hospital."

"I'm well aware." I tossed the blanket aside. It was too hot for a blanket. What was she thinking? "The doctor wouldn't have released me if I wasn't good to leave."

"At least rest today, please, Mom?"

Nate walked into the view of the sunroom windows. "Fine." A day on the couch watching Nate work wouldn't be the end of the world, especially if he removed his T-shirt.

Katie's gaze followed mine. "Who's that?"

"He's the contractor fixing the deck and painting the outside." Butterflies fluttered in my stomach.

"Why is he removing the deck?"

"It's rotten and needs replacing."

"Sounds like Dad," Katie scoffed.

"Katie!"

"What?" she grumbled and folded her arms.

"Sit down."

She ignored me. Joel walked into the room, observed the tense standoff, turned around, and left. No wonder Katie loved him so much. He was perfect for her.

"Please." I patted the couch cushion beside me.

She sunk onto the seat with her shoulders hunched, closing herself off to whatever I was about to say, but this had gone on long enough.

"Honey, what happened between me, and your dad wasn't your fault." I brushed her hair over her shoulder.

"I know." She picked at her fingers.

"It wasn't your dad's fault either. Or mine. It was no one's fault."

She opened her mouth.

"He may have cheated but truthfully we should have divorced years ago." I rested my hand on her back. "Don't let years go by holding this hurt inside. It's not good for you."

Katie's bottom lip quivered. "I'm sorry, Mom."

"Why are you sorry?" I asked with shock.

She shrugged. "For making this more difficult for you than it should be."

"Don't worry about me. I'm okay."

She twisted to face me. Her gaze roamed my face searching for the truth behind my words, and they were all true. I was okay.

"You look okay. Actually, you look amazing for someone who was bitten by a snake and spent time in the hospital."

"Thanks," I said, catching another glimpse of Nate. It surprised me to find myself longing to talk to him. "You and Joel should head off to work before you're late."

"I took the day off work."

"Why?"

"To look after you."

"But I don't need looking after."

"Tough. I'm spending the day waiting on you hand and foot like you used to do when I was a kid and home sick from school."

"But I'm not sick."

"Kate," Joel called from the doorway. "I'm off to work."

"Joel, talk sense into Katie. I don't need a babysitter."

Joel laughed. "I'm not getting in the middle of this."

"Wise move," Katie said and stood. She walked over to Joel and wrapped her arms around his neck. "I love you."

Joel beamed. "I love you too. Walk me to my car?"

My heart melted at their love. It was so beautiful to see and for them to share it with me. I was so happy Katie found someone as wonderful as Joel to fall in love with, and to think if it wasn't for Bosco and his never-ending naughtiness they may never have met.

Katie threw a warning look over her shoulder at me. I rolled my eyes. What did she imagine I'd get up to in such a short time?

Actually.

I stood and rushed to the French door and threw it open in a hurry. Nate's head snapped up from where he worked on the end of the deck.

"Hi, I'm home," I said, waving. I was an idiot. What was I doing?

Nate chuckled. "I can see. How are you?"

"Good, but Katie's insisting on playing nurse today."

"She sounds like a good kid."

"She is." I played with the door handle. "Thanks for everything you did yesterday." The front door shut with an echo. "I better sit before Nurse Katie finds me standing."

Nate nodded with his usual smile and happy lines dancing around his eyes, sending the butterflies in my stomach winging in happiness.

I rushed over to the couch and made it back before Katie walked into the room. I hid the slight tremble in my hands from talking to Nate under the blanket. "So, what are you planning for today?"

"We're starting with backgammon, then moving onto Scrabble when Aunt Hannah comes over."

"Hannah's coming over?"

"Yeah, she wants to make sure you rest too. She's upset you stepped in front of a snake for Bosco."

"I'd do it for any kid, and Bosco is like her child."

Katie laughed. "He is, isn't he?"

She left the room. I gazed out the window at Nate again. He was hard at work removing the timber boards. His arm muscles bulged, the veins popping out in the effort and the heat. Would it be wrong to pretend to be asleep so I could watch Nate?

Katie returned with the backgammon box and set the game on the coffee table.

"Can I get you anything?"

"No thanks, honey."

"Tell me if you're hungry or thirsty and I'll get it for you."

"You don't have to do this."

"Stop, Mom, and let me do this today, okay?"

"Okay," I said. "Okay."

"But the youngest still goes first." She rolled the dice.

I laughed and settled into a game of backgammon with my daughter.

Hannah walked in carrying a big white paper bag of delicious-smelling pastries. I eyed the Blissful Bites logo hungrily. Bosco followed with his nose in the air like Hannah was the Pied Piper.

She lifted the bags in the air. "I brought lunch."

"I can smell it," I said, standing from the couch, eager to get away from the never-ending backgammon games.

Hannah walked into the kitchen and extracted the individual bags from the big bag. One after another appeared. How many did she suppose would be at the house for lunch?

"I think I bought too much."

"You think?" I fetched glasses from the cupboard, but Katie walked over and took them out of my hand, and steered me toward the barstool.

"Would Nate like to join us?"

I paused with my bottom halfway to the stool. "Nate?"

"Who's Nate?" Katie asked.

"The hunky builder outside." Hannah waved her hands at the window. "I'll go ask him."

She disappeared before I objected. Katie set out four glasses and filled them with cool water and clinking ice cubes. She refilled the ice cube trays and kept busy, thank goodness. Imagine if she comprehended, I found Nate attractive.

Hannah came back with a triumphant smile on her face, and Nate followed behind her and behind him, Sampson.

"Hello," Nate said. "You must be Katie."

Katie smiled and ran her gaze over Nate from head to foot, then held out her hand.

Nate returned her smile. "Sorry, let me wash up first." He walked along the hallway toward the bathroom without being given directions.

Hannah and Katie examined me with a question in their eyes and raised eyebrows. I shifted on the stool, but Nate strode back into the kitchen before I explained. This looked bad for me.

Nate shook Katie's hand. "This is Sampson. He's deaf, so be careful touching him, otherwise, he startles if he doesn't see it coming."

Katie knelt for the dog. "Was he born deaf?"

"I assume he was. He's a rescue dog so there's no way of knowing for sure."

Katie gazed at Sampson with glistening eyes. "Hey, Sampson. I'm silly. You can't hear."

"Don't worry," Nate said. "Lots of people still talk to him. He seems to like it too."

Katie held her hand out for the dog. Sampson sniffed her knuckles and then lay on the floor. While Bosco on the other hand wandered around the kitchen sniffing everything for a crumb of food.

"Where shall we sit?" Katie stood.

"I set the dining room for four couples to eat. We can always shift the tables?"

"Here's good," Nate said and slid onto the barstool next to me. His leg brushed mine under the counter and sent a jolt of awareness skating over my skin.

"How's the deck looking?" I snatched the paper bag Hannah passed me.

"Half destroyed." Nate chuckled. "I've ordered the new timber, and they'll deliver it next Monday. Plenty of time for me to deconstruct the old one."

"Are you building it the same?" Katie asked.

"Similar, but Madeline had great ideas to improve the deck and make it cozy, so we decided to go with them."

His words sounded way more intimate than they should.

I chomped on the sausage roll. Flakes of pastry fell to the bench top, and I wiped them onto the floor for Bosco to lick. Nate picked up a bag and took a bite of his sausage roll too. Katie and Hannah ate as well, and the room fell into a half-uncomfortable silence.

Hannah fed pieces of her sausage roll to Bosco. Nate shook his head and slid a card from his shorts pocket.

"Here's the card for the dog trainer." He handed Hannah a small rectangle of black paper with a golden dog on the front.

"Thank you." Hannah turned the card over and read the details on the back. "Carter's Canine Control. 1623 Longview Drive, Paradise Point. That's not far."

"No, it's about a fifteen-minute drive," I said.

"When did you go to Paradise Point?" Katie asked.

"Ah, was it Friday or Saturday I was at your house?" I peered at Nate.

Katie and Hannah's mouths fell open.

"It was Friday after we first met."

"That's right, how could I forget?" I grinned remembering the way he'd come to my rescue on the deck.

"Mom," Katie whispered. "You were at his house?"

"His office is at his house. It's a beautiful place too. Right on the hilltop overlooking the beach. The view is spectacular." I tucked my hair behind my ear.

"Thanks, Madeline. Your view is beautiful too."

"I like it here." I waved to the kitchen window and the magnificent view of the white sand beach and sapphire blue surf beyond. Surfers dotted the horizon and sent envy through my limbs at the freedom they must experience on the waves. It was time I faced my fear and took my surfboard out into the water.

"I need a glass of wine," Katie mumbled.

"There's a fresh box in the laundry."

Katie left the room in a hurry. Bosco trotted after her. He still loved Katie even after she almost killed him with a chocolate mud cake. Not that it was her fault entirely. Bosco ate anything he got his snout near.

I finished my pastry and crumpled the paper bag into a ball while Nate did the same thing at the same time. We gazed at each other and laughed.

Katie returned with a bottle of wine in one hand and a man's T-shirt in the other. Her eyebrows disappeared into her hair in a disbelieving look on her face.

"Oh, good, you've got Nate's T-shirt. Sorry, I keep forgetting to give it back to you."

Katie handed the top to Nate and sat on the stool with a thump.

Nate stood and tucked the T-shirt into his back pocket. My gaze dipped to his tight ass, then snapped up to his face.

"Thanks for lunch. I'd better get back to work since the deck won't rip itself apart."

We all watched Nate leave the kitchen with Sampson obediently by his side.

"Well," Hannah said. "My next novel needs a hunky construction worker."

I giggled. Seriously, what's with my giggling? Am I forty-two or twelve?

Katie folded her arms. "I don't want to ask this, but, Mom, why was his T-shirt in your laundry?"

I pointed a finger. "Not what you're thinking, but I'm not telling how or why because it's too embarrassing for me."

"Now I need to know." Hannah rubbed her hands together. "More book fodder."

"No." I shook my head. "Let's just say it involved Bosco. Who's up for Scrabble?"

Hannah sighed. "How will I ever get my spark back unless you help me?"

I stood and patted her shoulder. "I'm sure you'll find a way."

Chapter Eleven

I eyed the surfboard. I could do this. Maybe? I'd put it off too long. It was time I learned how to surf. I lived on one of the best surf beaches in Western Australia, and I'd purchased the board the moment the house contract was completed, but I hadn't entered the water on it. I was anxious I'd make an absolute idiot of myself.

Nothing like an almost near-death experience to make me realize life's too short to procrastinate.

I struggled with the surfboard to the water's edge and placed it in the sparkling sapphire blue water. The waves bobbed the board. It looked scarier this close. I should just sit on it for today and get a sense of the movement.

I inched into the water and sat on the board with my toes touching the wet sand underneath. This wasn't too bad. The caress of the waves washed over my legs and splashed up onto the board. Luckily the water was warm even in the morning.

Thank goodness Katie went to work at her office. It'd surprised both of us with the amount of work she'd received when people heard an accountant had moved into town. It would leave me to run the bed-and-breakfast by myself, but I didn't mind, so long as my daughter was happy, and she was. Apart from her relationship with her dad.

The sun grew warmer the longer I sat on the board. More people ventured onto the beach. I probably looked stupid, but I didn't care. I lifted my face to the sky and gazed at the soft, fluffy white clouds rolling across the cornflower blue. This was good.

I glanced back down at the tropical purple palm tree pattern on the surfboard. Could I stand on the board and not fall off? I lifted my legs. The board wobbled. No. I put my legs back down until my toes touched the sand. Baby steps. Just like teaching Katie to walk. One step at a time and this step was enough for today.

I slid off the board and dunked myself under the salty water. Then I dragged the surfboard from the waves and struggled my way up the white sand back to my beach house with it in my arms.

Nate smiled in greeting having started work while the water and surfboard had preoccupied me.

"Good morning."

"Good morning." I couldn't stop the smile forming on my lips at the sight of Nate. The butterflies fluttered with happiness to see him too.

Nate's gaze roamed the length of my swimsuit-clad body. Where were his trademark sunglasses? My body reacted with tingles to his appraisal.

"Interesting way to surf."

"I'll let you in on a secret," I said, leaning closer, "I don't know how."

"You're kidding? I'd never guess."

I giggled. Again, with the giggling. I pinched my arm and stood up straight.

"I can teach you if you like?"

"You know how to surf?" His body appeared fit for surfing, but he'd never mentioned he surfed.

"Yes, I know how to surf. If you're interested, I'd be happy to teach you."

"Well...I...oh...um...sure, why not?"

He laughed. "Is that a yes?"

"Yes." I laughed with him.

"Tomorrow morning work for you? Before I work on your deck?"

"Perfect. I can pay you."

"No, you're not paying me. I offered."

"But—"

"No." He folded his arms.

"Thanks, Nate. I appreciate it. I'd love to learn how to surf with your help."

"It'll be my pleasure."

Don't blush. I tucked my damp hair behind my ears.

"I'm planning to try another muffin recipe today. Would you mind being a guinea pig again?" I wriggled my toes in the soft, warm sand.

"Absolutely."

"Great. I'll see you at lunch." My lips spread into a cheerful grin. I hefted the surfboard into my arms and made my way to the front door. I'd be glad when Nate had rebuilt the deck, and I could use the back door again, but then I wouldn't see Nate every day...

The next morning Nate waited for me at the water's edge. The waves were nonexistent today. A flat calm enveloped the bay, but not me. I was so nervous about learning to surf. How would I learn with no waves?

"Morning," I snapped.

Nate turned from the spectacular view of the water and smiled. "Good morning."

I dropped the surfboard on the sand. "I can't do this."

"Relax. Yes, you can." He picked up my hands. "We'll take this slow, okay? There's no need to rush, and days like today are perfect for complete beginners."

"What, surfing with no waves?" Any other time I'd lose all brainwaves when he touched me, but I was way too nervous about learning to surf.

"Yes. What you did yesterday was great, learning to handle the movement of the board in the water. It's what every beginner should do. We'll do that again today, and I'll teach you a few things on the sand."

"No standing on the board in the water?"

"Not yet. Basics first. Are you worried about standing on the board in the water?"

"I am. It looks positively hair-raising."

He squeezed my hands. "Yet here you are willing to try."

I dipped my head and finally enjoyed the warmth of his hands on mine. They were rough and calloused from his hard work against the softness of my hands. A tingle started from my palms and traveled up my arms.

"Let's do this." Why was I so scared? It's just water, and with Nate's presence, I felt like I could do anything.

Nate let go of my hands and kneeled next to the surfboard.

"A few fundamentals first. This is the deck." He ran a hand over the front of the surfboard with the palm tree pattern.

Sudden imaginings of his hand running over my back popped into my head.

"The sides are the rails." He gripped the sides of the board with both hands.

Now I imagined him gripping my sides.

He flipped the board over. "Fins."

"Like a fish," I joked. Willing my imaginings to not think about him flipping me over.

"Yep, they give you direction in the water."

"Nose." He tapped the top of the surfboard then the bottom. "Tail."

"Got it."

"This here is your leg rope. You attach the strap to your back foot."

I frowned. "Both my feet are the same."

Nate chuckled. "When you stand, one foot will be in front of the other and the leg rope goes on the ankle of the foot at the tail of the board."

"Oh, right." He must think I'm a complete idiot.

"Come stand on the board." He patted the deck.

I padded across the white sand and stepped onto the board with both feet next to each other. Nate tapped a finger to my left ankle.

"Shuffle this foot back to the tail."

I did as he said.

"Turn your foot a little like this." He wrapped his fingers around my ankle and repositioned my foot. "How does that feel?"

"Ah...yeah...good."

Don't blush. He asked about my position, not the way his hand touched my leg. Both were good, but the way he wrapped his fingers around my ankle had my heart palpitating in a wild rhythm of excitement.

"Try the stance the other way around."

I shuffled on the board and changed my position. "Like this?"

"Perfect." He grinned. "Which one is better?"

I shrugged. "The first one."

"All right, we'll work with that stance. but first I want you to lie on the board."

I eased my way on to the deck. Weird calling the surfboard a deck like it's a boat or something.

"Wriggle back a bit. You don't want to be too far forward or back."

I wriggled down the board. My swimsuit crept higher up my buttocks with my movements. This was way too sexual with Nate watching me. I couldn't very well extract my bathing suit with his gaze on me. I'd have to suffer the wedgie for now.

Nate cleared his throat. "See the line in the middle of the board? That's the center. Make sure you're lined up with the line and you won't have any problems with falling off while paddling."

"Paddling?" I turned my head to Nate. "Like a dog?"

"Maddy, you're so much fun." He chuckled. "Cup your hands like this and when you're out on the water laying on the board, you swing your arms over like this with big, long strokes, and propel yourself through the water."

I copied Nate, trying to not hit the sand with my swings. I didn't succeed and flicked sand up at Nate's face.

He brushed the grains from his brow. "Let's try in the water."

"Okay." I jumped up only causing my wedgie to ride up further. I wriggled, but my bathing suit was stuck.

"Pick up the board from the nose and take it out into the water." He stripped his T-shirt over his head.

Every brainwave left my mind being this close to his topless perfection. What did he say? That's right. I bent over in a rush before he caught me checking him out, yet again. Oh, good grief. I may as well be wearing a thong swimsuit. Why did I have this wardrobe malfunction today with Nate watching? I dragged the board into the water in a hurry. Once we were waist-deep, I yanked my swimsuit free from my crevice.

"You good?" Nate asked seeing my discomfort.

"Yes, yes. Now what?"

"Now I want you to lie on the board and experience the way it travels in the water."

"That's it?"

"For today. It's the most important thing to learn, the motion of the water, because not one wave is the same. This amazing water playground is constantly changing. The wind, tides, and swell all affect the way the board travels. When you can feel it, really feel it, you'll love surfing as much as I do."

"That's beautiful, Nate." I wriggled onto the surfboard in a very unspectacular fashion and shifted into the position he taught me on the beach. "Do you surf often?"

"Not as much as I used to." He held on to the surfboard for me and gazed out at the flat sea.

"Why not?"

"Oliver went through a few issues two years ago and I cut back then to help him through them."

"Is he okay?"

"He's better. Oliver got caught up in the wrong crowd and started drinking. He's clean now and no longer associates with that crowd, but I worry about him. He doesn't know what he wants to do with his future. It's hard being a parent."

"I'm sorry he experienced that." I placed my fingers on top of his. "He's lucky to have a wonderful father like you."

Nate glanced at our fingers and sank into the water up to his shoulders, so he bobbed at eye level with me.

"You're something else, Madeline, you know that?"

I blushed. His intense gaze roamed my face, which was so hot I probably looked like a beetroot. I licked my lips tasting the salty tang of the water. Nate's gaze followed the motion.

"No being inappropriate while I'm employed by you," he muttered and stood.

The water dripped from his shirtless body in rivers I wanted to follow with my tongue. Guess I was the one having inappropriate imaginings. I shifted uncomfortably on the board. The action caused the surfboard to wobble, and I toppled from the side into the water. I rose with a splutter of salty lips and giggled.

Nate threw his head back and laughed.

I liked Nate, more than I should as his employer. More than I should as a still married woman.

Chapter Twelve

The week flew by. I spent mornings on the beach with Nate learning how to surf. Then I'd pretend not to watch him work on my deck, which he'd torn to pieces now, and was ready for the delivery of new timber on Monday.

I'd tried a new muffin recipe each day, to Nate's eager appetite and glowing praise. Even Hannah and Katie liked my muffins, though in secret I made them for Nate first, but they didn't know that.

Then, Katie, Joel, and Hannah would arrive for dinner where I'd practice more recipes for my soon-to-be bed-and-breakfast. My days fell into a pleasant routine, and I was happy with my life in Hope Bay.

Until the weekend rolled around and on Saturday, I missed seeing Nate and his smiling face. I moped like a sulky toddler. On Sunday, Joel and Katie left for a drive into Perth to go shopping. Hannah ignored my plea to keep me company and said she'd be writing.

Sunday loomed long and boring. I could go out by myself. I didn't need company. I should be happy by myself. A minute later, I was in my car and driving to who knows where before I knew it.

Except my path took me to our silk farm, well, not ours now, my ex-husband's, who still wasn't my ex. We needed to sort out our divorce. I drove up the driveway to the entrance of the farm under the swinging metal sign. I shouldn't have come on a Sunday—it was peak tourist time—but I wanted to get Garry to sign the joint application divorce papers. He'd had the papers for weeks now.

I parked in the packed parking lot and walked over to the gift shop. Whoever manned the shop now would know where I could find Garry on the farm. I opened the door and rolled my eyes. She stood behind the counter—the young, flirty woman who'd had an affair with my husband. Women like her gave other women terrible names.

I yanked my handbag strap higher onto my shoulder and marched up to the counter. Guess I held a bit of anger about the affair.

"Marsha, where's Garry?" He even picked a woman with the same initial. I bet it was so that when he mixed up the names, he could cover himself.

Marsha had the good grace to look uncomfortable. She glanced around the shop at the customers. Did she expect me to yell or something? She didn't know me too well. It wasn't worth yelling over. Neither of them was worth my time or energy.

"He's out the back in the learning center with a bunch of kids. You don't want to disturb him."

I narrowed my eyes. Of all the nerve! "I don't want to disturb him, do I, Marsha? I know more about how to run the silk farm than you."

My gaze ran over her youthful form. Garry could have at least had better judgment for whom he left me. Marsha was a straight-up gold digger. Before Garry, she'd attempted to lure the wine yard neighbor's husband into an affair, but he loved his wife. The same couldn't be said for my soon-to-be ex-husband.

I stomped out of the gift shop and past the small cafeteria seated with an abundance of families. It was good to see the farm doing well. I crossed my fingers my new bed-and-breakfast business would do this well. Otherwise, it would hurt that I'd helped make the silk farm a success.

Families filled the learning center with eager young children listening to Garry in his khaki uniform. I stood at the back of the spacious room and leaned on the wall. He was good at his job, I'd give him that. His gaze flicked to mine in surprise, then he smiled. Surely, he wasn't happy to see me.

I folded my arms and waited for Garry to finish his talk. When he did, he shook hands with parents, patted kids on the back, and gave the impression of a good guy. He was a good guy, just not a good husband.

As the room cleared, he ventured over to me. "Madeline, what are you doing here?"

I checked no one was close, unfolded my arms, and stood up straight. "Garry, sign the divorce papers."

He stepped closer. "Can we not do this here and now?"

"When then?" I tapped my foot. "You've had the papers for weeks. We've been separated for nearly two years. You're in a relationship with someone else. What's the holdup?"

He grabbed my elbow and steered me out of the learning center. "I've been meaning to talk to you."

"So, talk."

"Not here." He glanced around. "Can I come to see you?"

"So long as you bring the divorce papers with you."

He walked with me to the entrance of the farm with a glower etched on his face. I spun away from him and walked to my car without a backward glance. He was so frustrating. I'd wasted too many years with Garry, and I should have moved on sooner. I should never have been around when he found a younger woman to take my place.

Lesson learned. And learned hard. No more putting someone else's happiness first. My life was about me. Me and my happiness. Garry wouldn't bring me down ever again.

I drove away from the silk farm knowing I'd never set foot on it again and realizing it didn't matter to me. My life was in Hope Bay. A joyful life, full of fun, adventure, and laughter.

On the way back home—yes, the beach house was my *home*—I stopped at The Seaside Jewel and ordered a delicious tuna and salad wrap for lunch. I soaked in the atmosphere of my hometown and the pleasure of my company. A silly grin stretched across my lips. Funny how closure finds you when you least expect it.

I was soon to be a divorcee.

Soon to be single.

Soon to be a bed-and-breakfast owner and operator.

Soon to be a surfer.

Nate's smiling face and gentle encouragement drifted into my mind. We'd formed a solid friendship in a week. Another funny thing how that had happened. What would happen between us when he'd finished the work on my beach house?

I'd make sure we stayed friends. Besides, there were still plenty of surf lessons he needed to give me. I was certain I wouldn't be a confident surfer by the time he'd finished working on the house. I could always take Bosco for playdates with Sampson too if Hannah let me.

"Hi, Madeline, how are the renovations going?" Bree asked, stopping by my table with her girlfriend, Lucy.

"Fantastic. It shouldn't be long now until I'll be able to open it. Just waiting for the contractor to replace the deck and paint the outside."

Bree waved to Alley. Alley and her famous surfer boyfriend, Kai Scott, wandered across from the doorway.

"I spotted you on the beach the other day having surf lessons. Good on you. I've never been game to learn," Bree said.

"I hope you've got a good teacher," Kai said. "The most important thing to learn about is ocean awareness, surf safety, wave etiquette, and proper technique."

"Yes, thanks, Kai, Nate has been teaching me all that and how not to surf alone, and to check the weather and wave predictions before heading out."

"Good. A local would be better as they know the area. I can teach you while I'm in town."

Alley gazed at Kai adoringly.

"That's okay, Kai, Nate's local enough, he lives in Paradise Point." Besides, I couldn't imagine anyone else teaching me how to surf. It embarrassed and thrilled me with Nate teaching me.

"Wouldn't be Nate Hudson by any chance?"

"Yes, that's him. Do you know Nate?"

Kai grinned. "I know Nate. He's an amazing surfer. You're in excellent hands with him as your teacher."

"Good to know."

Kai whispered in Alley's ear. Alley's eyes widened and then she grinned too.

"Kai is a good teacher too." Alley kissed Kai's cheek.

A new love was sweet, and these two couples had definitely found love. My heart sang with joy to see them all so happy. It also reaffirmed the notion love was attainable. At forty-two I wasn't too old for love.

They all joined me at the table, and we ordered a round of drinks. Alley and Bree regaled us with doggy tales from The Pooch Parlor which made us all laugh out loud. Not surprisingly, Bosco was the dog with the most tales.

As lunch rolled into mid-afternoon, we all left tipsy and in all that time I'd never felt like the fifth wheel. Everyone in Hope Bay was so friendly and welcoming.

I left my car at The Seaside Jewel and wandered home along the beach. Tourists sunbathed on the pristine sand, their skin varying from shades of light pink to burnt lobster, despite that, they persisted. People's heads bobbed in the sparkling blue water as they swam and played. A few surfers hit the small waves further along the beach away from the swimmers. The salty tang of the breeze teased my lips and ruffled my hair. I slid my shoes from my feet and sunk my toes into the warm sand.

A deep sigh left my entire body.

Contentment washed over me.

This place had a way of soothing my soul.

Of mending everything I didn't realize needed fixing inside me.

I lifted my face to the sun and continued home. I'd walk back later tonight and collect my car when I'd sobered enough to drive, or I'd collect a bottle of wine from home and sit on the beach to watch the sunset.

The perfect way to end the day.

Chapter Thirteen

I slid sunglasses on, regretting the bottle of wine. I didn't even attempt to fix my hair after dragging myself out of bed for my surf lesson.

"Are you okay?" Nate asked with concern.

I held up my forefinger and thumb. "A wee bit hungover."

Nate laughed. I cringed.

"Come on," he said taking my hand. "Leave the board for today and let's take a relaxing dip. It's an excellent cure for a hangover."

I slunk into the water like a sea slug returning to the sea.

We sat in the cool water. The waves lapped gently against my chest. Birds chirped somewhere in the distance. Thank goodness they weren't close. After many minutes, the water eased my pounding head and goosebumps erupted on my arms.

"You'll need to buy a wetsuit soon. The water is cooling."

"I can't think of anything worse. They look so...so...fitted." I screwed up my nose pondering how tight they adhered to bodies. I wouldn't look good in one. A wetsuit would show my bulges.

"You have nothing to worry about. You'll look hot in one."
He held up his hands. "Sorry, inappropriate. Let's change the
subject. Were you celebrating last night?"

"Oh, no. Nothing to celebrate unless you count me
confronting my husband about signing the divorce application
papers."

"And did he?"

"No, not yet, apparently he wants to talk first. I'm sure it's
about Katie, but I've tried talking to her multiple times about
her dad. What else can I do? She's a grown woman with a mind
of her own, and if she doesn't want to see her dad, how am I
meant to make her?" I babbled like an idiot. "Sorry, I didn't
mean to unload on you."

"Not a problem. I've unloaded on you too."

"Not like I did." I frowned. Why was Nate so easy to talk to?

"You're right about Katie. You can only talk to her and let
her decide for herself. It must be hard for her having her parents
separate after you've been together so long."

"I can't imagine. My parents have always been together. It's
probably why I didn't leave Garry. I didn't want to disappoint
them."

"Mine too. Dad ran the construction business until I took
over. Now he's happily retired and spending all his time with
Mom. It's sweet. How's your hangover now?"

"Better, thanks." And it was. The mere presence of Nate
eased my aching head and not the cool water.

"So, my son is coming to help me today. I hope you don't
mind."

"Why would I mind?" I swirled my hands in the water.

"Surly teenager and all that."

I snickered. "I've been through the stage, remember."

"Right, well, if you have any suggestions..."

I shrugged. "Why shouldn't you suffer like every parent
ever?"

"Harsh." He flicked water at me with his fingers.

I flicked the water back and giggled. Nate's eyes narrowed. Then he sank under the water. I squawked and swam out deeper. Nate caught me easily. He wrapped an arm around my waist, and we bobbed in the water together. I kicked my feet to stay afloat while Nate seemed relaxed.

He brushed a water drop running down my cheek. A zing of awareness traveled along my skin. His naked chest registered squashed against mine. My chest heaved as excitement and the intense attraction of this man holding me hit me with the full force of what I'd been ignoring.

God, he was gorgeous, and he looked at me like he believed I was the gorgeous one. My heart beat wildly while the butterflies took flight. Maybe one kiss...

The sun glinted off my gold wedding ring as my hand rested on his shoulder.

No. I couldn't do it. Yet. Not until I took this band from my finger. The moment I did though, and Nate finished working for me, I might do something crazy like kiss Nate.

Or it might be idiotic, and I'd ruin our friendship.

I eased out of his arms and swam back to shore. With a glance over my shoulder, I said, "I'll make extra muffins for lunch today. Teenagers are always hungry."

Nate followed me with a curious expression dragging his usual smile from his face.

Was he having the same imaginings as me? It sure felt like he was as attracted to me as I was to him. Time would tell.

Nate and his son worked hard all morning carrying the new timber boards from the front of the beach house and building the new framework. The constant pound of nailing echoed through the house. Thank goodness my hangover disappeared after our refreshing swim. I switched on the radio and danced and sang to music while cooking a batch of muffins. Zucchini and cheddar this time.

Before I'd time to call the boys in, Nate knocked on the front door.

"Smells delicious, as usual." Nate stepped inside. "This is Oliver, my son."

I recognized him as the checkout operator.

"Hi, Oliver." I held out my hand. Now I understood why he'd seemed familiar at the supermarket.

The teenager stared at my hand like it was a foreign object before reluctantly shaking it.

"Call me Madeline. You work at the supermarket, don't you?"

"Yeah, you bought dog treats the other week."

"I did." I shut the door behind them.

"Where's your dog?" Oliver scanned the house.

He was similar in looks to his dad, with shoulder-length brown hair and the build of a surfer. He probably had a ton of girls chasing after him if he didn't have a girlfriend.

"I don't have one. I was dog-sitting my sister's dog."

His face fell.

"No Sampson today?" I asked Nate.

"No, I left him home. He has an aversion to the nail gun."

"I understand his pain, it's rather loud. Oh, I'm an idiot, he's deaf."

Oliver snickered. Nate nudged him with his elbow.

I smiled. "Don't mind me, Oliver, I still haven't learned to not put my foot in my mouth sometimes. Go wash up and meet me in the kitchen."

The boy nodded and followed Nate.

Surly teenager, check. A like for dogs, check. Tomorrow I'd see if Hannah could bring Bosco over for the boy.

They met me in the kitchen where I poured them tall glasses of iced water and handed them a plate with a muffin each. They muttered their thanks and tucked in.

When they finished, I asked, "Well?"

"Delicious as usual." Nate grabbed another muffin.

Oliver avoided looking at me.

"Oliver, what did you think? And be honest—I'm experimenting with flavors for my future guests."

"It's okay," he mumbled.

"Just okay?" I frowned. "What didn't you like?"

"I liked it. It's heavy on the zucchini. Next time you should strain the liquid from the zucchini so they're not so soggy."

"They're soggy?" I picked up a muffin and bit into it. Instantly I grasped what Oliver meant. "You're right, Oliver, these aren't very good."

Nate nudged Oliver with his elbow.

"I didn't mean that," he mumbled.

"No, that's okay. I appreciate your honesty." I put down the muffin. "Would you mind helping me remake them tomorrow? If your dad doesn't mind me stealing you for an hour."

Nate's eyes widened.

"Is it okay, Dad?" Oliver turned to Nate.

"Sure, if you'd like to help Madeline, you can."

"Yeah, I'd like that." Oliver twisted back to me. "Have you considered using another cheese?"

"No, I haven't. What do you suggest? I need to pick up my car so I can fetch new ingredients."

"Where's your car?" Nate asked.

"I left my car at The Seaside Jewel yesterday." I shrugged. "One shouldn't drink and drive."

Oliver snickered. Nate nudged him with his elbow again.

"No, you shouldn't drink and drive," Nate agreed.

"So, what ingredients am I buying, Oliver?"

Oliver leaned forward on the bar and excitedly launched into a discussion on the merits and drawbacks of using unique cheeses in the muffin mix. Nate sat back with an amused expression on his face and scratched his beard. Then he threw me a smile that made my butterflies soar.

The following day, I discovered Oliver was a closet budding chef. He came alive in the kitchen mixing and stirring, talking about tastes, textures, and consistency. He'd found his calling and didn't realize it yet.

Nate threw us curious glances from outside while he worked on the deck. I could sense his desire to come into the kitchen and watch, but he left us to it. When I waved the muffins were ready, he was at the front door in no time.

"I'm impressed, Oliver," Nate said licking his fingers. "These muffins are the best thing I've ever tasted."

I folded my arms and pretended to scowl.

Nate swallowed. "No offense, Madeline, your muffins are great too."

I giggled and Oliver snickered.

"Way to backpedal, Dad."

Nate held up his hands. "Are you two ganging up on me?"

Oliver and I exchanged glances, then laughed again.

"I was thinking, Oliver," I said. "I'll be opening my bed-and-breakfast soon and I can use an extra pair of hands with my daughter Katie working full time now. Would you like a part-time job here?"

Nate's mouth fell open.

Oliver beamed. "I'd like that."

"I'm not sure about hours yet, but I can ask Bailey or the owners of The Seaside Jewel if they have any positions vacant too. With your cooking skills, we can find you plenty of work in Hope Bay."

Oliver squared his grey T-shirt-clad shoulders and grew a foot taller. Nate blinked rapidly and patted Oliver on the back. For the rest of lunch, Oliver and I talked about food and potential menu items for the bed-and-breakfast. Then he glimpsed the time.

"We should get back to work on the deck, Dad."

Nate smiled. "Yeah, can you get started? I'd like to talk to Madeline for a moment."

"Sure thing." Oliver left the kitchen with a new strut to his strides.

Nate slid off his stool and rounded the counter. I stepped back until my bottom hit the wall, but Nate kept coming. He stopped a hairsbreadth away from me.

"I could seriously kiss you right now." His gaze dipped to my lips.

The butterflies in my stomach fluttered in excitement.

"But that'd be inappropriate," he mumbled.

"Totally," I whispered, dropping my gaze to his lips.

"You're something else, Madeline." He placed a hand on the wall next to my head. "I've never seen Oliver so excited about anything. Thank you."

"You're welcome." I brushed my hair back from my face and tucked the strands behind my ear.

"Maddy," he groaned and pushed off the wall. "I can't wait until I'm no longer employed by you."

He strutted from the kitchen in the same way Oliver did, the resemblance clear in every step. I sank against the wall and held a hand to my stomach. I hoped like anything they'd finish the deck and painting sooner than quoted because I wanted to know what Nate's kiss was like.

But then I was still married. I twisted my wedding ring. I couldn't kiss Nate until Garry signed the divorce papers.

Chapter Fourteen

T hree weeks later, Nate completed the deck. He'd surpassed my expectations of cozy. The bench seats were perfect for sitting on and watching the calm serenity of the beach and waves. I loved the new deck more than the original.

He only had the painting of the exterior of the beach house to complete. Butterflies floated around my stomach on a daily, sometimes hourly, basis. Oliver was wonderful in the kitchen, and I'd found him part-time work at The Seaside Jewel a few nights a week. Nate was always complimenting me on how much I'd helped Oliver. I'd brushed it off, but it meant a lot to Nate to see his son happy, but I understood how he felt as I enjoyed seeing my daughter happy.

I peered out the kitchen window watching Nate work. It was all I did lately. He jerked his T-shirt over his head and wiped the sweat from his brow, then hung the T-shirt over the rail of the deck. It wasn't like I didn't see him every day without a top while he taught me to surf, but I leaned closer to the window.

"Are the seals back?" Katie walked into the kitchen. She and Joel were taking the day off work together.

"What?" I spun around. "Ah, no."

But Katie had already joined me at the window.

"Ah," she muttered then slung an arm around my shoulder and turned me back to the view of Nate working topless. "You're enjoying *that* view."

"Katie." I wriggled uncomfortably under her arm.

"What?" She shrugged. "I've gotten used to the idea, now. It blindsided me when I first met him, but you two are great together. Are you dating?"

"No, we're not dating." I held up my left hand. "I'm still married."

"Mom, Dad has moved on, you should too."

"Sorry, I can't date while I'm married. It'd be wrong."

Katie's lips firmed into a tight line.

"Besides," I said. "Nate's way too young for me."

"How old is he?"

I shrugged. I wouldn't tell her I knew his age and how he was eight years younger than me.

"Are you ready to go?" Joel wandered into the room.

"In a minute," Katie said without turning from the window. Concentration lines marred her face.

"What's so interesting on the beach?" Joel joined us at the window, grasped Nate was the only thing on the beach, then laughed. "I'll wait in the car."

Katie swiped my phone from the counter.

"What are you doing?"

She tapped away at the screen. "I'm finding out how old Nate is."

"Wait, you don't need to..."

"Oh," she gasped.

See, he was too young for me.

"He's too young, I know." I hung my head.

"No, it's not that." She turned the phone, so I could see the screen.

"Oh," I gasped in the same way Katie did.

Then we both swung to the window. Joel stood chatting with Nate, then they turned our way. I dropped to the floor in a hurry. My face heated to an inferno. This was way too embarrassing. Getting caught staring, and...

Katie glanced down at me and grinned.

"Shh." I touched a finger to my lips while I stared at the phone screen in my hand and the image of Nate.

"Madeline, what are you doing down there?" Nate asked.

I jumped and dropped my phone. It skittered away on the tiled floor with a clatter. Lucky for me my phone didn't break. Katie left the room in a hurry. Nate bent and picked up my phone, glancing at the screen as he handed it to me.

"I guess you know."

I couldn't move. My body had frozen in place. This was way too humiliating for me.

"Why didn't you say anything?" I rasped.

He rolled his shoulders and slunk to the floor next to me.

"It was a lifetime ago, and I didn't want to intimidate you. I wanted to teach you how to surf."

"But you were a professional surfer."

"I was. I'm not now."

"Still..."

"Still what?" He plucked the phone from my hand and flicked through the images of himself surfing.

"Why would you want to teach me how to surf when you can do that?" I touched the screen, and the image grew bigger.

Nate was magnificent on the board. His hair streaming behind him. He was clean-shaven in the photo and appeared even younger. The wetsuit clung to his toned form. The wave was huge, like a mountain behind him, yet he smiled with such happiness.

"Why did you give up surfing? You look so happy."

"I was, but Oliver wasn't happy with me being away so much." He shrugged.

"Will you go back to pro surfing now that Oliver's happy?" I held my breath waiting for his answer. In the short time, we'd known each other, he'd become an important friend to me, and maybe one day we'd be more if I ever got divorced and stopped worrying about our age gap.

"No." He shook his head. "I'm ready for the next stage of my life."

His gaze pierced mine and then dropped to my lips.

"I..." I stood in a hurry before I gave in to the desire to kiss him.

Nate stood with a sigh and handed me my phone. Our fingers touched sending sparks of excitement thrumming through my veins.

"I'll get back to work. I'll finish painting tomorrow if the weather holds. There's a storm off the coast and it might head this way."

"Really? I've never been through a storm on the coast."

"You're in for a treat if we get a lightning show."

We had a lightning show of our own whenever we touched.

"Will it be okay for my surfing lesson tomorrow?" I clenched my phone. After practicing the pop-up on the sand on the board and only one attempt in the water, I didn't want to try if the waves were big.

"Should be fine, but I'll check the weather reports in the morning and let you know if we need to cancel."

"Thanks, Nate, and thanks for teaching me to surf. I can't believe a pro surfer is teaching me." I shook my head. All this time I'd been learning to surf with a famous surfer. Suddenly Kai's comment made sense. No wonder he knew Nate. They most likely surfed in the same competitions.

Nate chuckled. "I'm just a contractor now."

Nate wandered out of the kitchen. He was anything but a contractor. He was... I glared at my wedding ring. I'd never hated the band so much.

Misty-grey clouds brimmed the morning sky. I tugged on my new black wetsuit. The material clung to my form. I couldn't wait to show Nate my new purchase. It was right for me to buy one after learning he was a pro surfer, teaching little old me.

A loud rap of knuckles resonated on the front door. Did it mean he'd cancel the surf lesson? Is that why Nate knocked on the front door instead of waiting for me on the beach? I hurried through the house, swung the door open, and stepped back in shock.

"Garry?"

"What are you wearing?" He stepped into the house uninvited.

"A wetsuit." I folded my arms. "Why are you here?"

"I told you I would come."

"Yes, but you should've called first."

"Like you did when you appeared at the silk farm?"

I clenched my fists. "It's a public place. I have every right to visit the farm like any person."

We eyed each other.

Garry huffed. "I didn't come here to argue with you."

"Then why are you here?" I unfolded my arms.

"Can we do this somewhere other than your hallway?"

"Come into the kitchen and I'll make coffee." I led the way to the kitchen. It felt wrong with Garry here invading my space. My home. Like my house and I rejected his presence.

Garry settled onto the stool Nate usually sat on when eating the muffins at lunch. The wrongness grew. I slid a coffee across the counter and kept my distance.

"You look good." Garry picked up his mug and sipped.

"Thanks, I guess." In all our years of marriage, I could count the number of times he said I looked good on one hand.

"Have you lost weight?"

"None of your business, Garry." I grabbed the cloth and wiped the counter, needing something to do with my hands.

"I suppose." He stared at his mug.

"Why are you here?" I asked again.

"I wanted to talk to you before I sign these." He stood and withdrew an envelope from his jacket pocket.

Oh, thank goodness, he'd brought the joint application divorce papers. About time too.

"There's not much to talk about. Our marriage is over."

He grimaced and then sipped his coffee. "Katie called me."

"She did?" I rose my eyebrows. "That's good."

"She said you were happy, and I should sign the papers for you."

"I am happy, and you should." I threw the cloth into the sink behind me. "It's the least you can do for me. For us."

"We were happy together."

"Sometimes, Garry, we were, but we were more comfortable."

"I liked our comfort." He gulped the rest of his coffee. "I made a mistake."

"Garry." I sighed. "You did, and you didn't. You shouldn't have cheated, but you ended our marriage when I couldn't."

"Did you want to end it?"

I dipped my head. "We both did and were too scared to admit it."

"I miss you sometimes."

I sighed. "That there, Garry tells you everything. You only miss me sometimes. If you loved me, you'd miss me all the time."

He withdrew the papers from the envelope. I handed him a pen, and he signed the divorce papers. I expected to experience something, anything, but I had no regret, or sadness, no happiness or excitement. Just a moment of end.

I slid my wedding ring from my finger and walked around the counter and placed the gold band on the divorce papers. Garry picked up the ring and stood.

"Thank you," I said. "For everything."

Garry held out his arms, and I stepped into them. I hoped this amicable end to our marriage would heal the rift between him and Katie. I stepped back from Garry ready to start my life as a divorcee.

Chapter Fifteen

"Sorry I'm late," I called to Nate on the beach and hurried the rest of the way to the stormy-blue water's edge.

Nate didn't turn.

I dropped the board in the sand and touched his shoulder. He stepped away, so my hand hung in mid-air.

"We won't have much time now, perhaps we should cancel."

"But I purchased a wetsuit," I said with a wave of my hand up and down my body. "What do you think?"

His gaze barely registered my wetsuit. "It's a good fit."

"Are you okay?"

"Yeah, why wouldn't I be?"

"I don't know." I shrugged. But the normally happy, smiling Nate wasn't here today.

"I'm just in a hurry to finish the painting before the weather turns."

"Oh, okay." I dropped my gaze to the sand.

"Sorry, Madeline. How about you do a couple of runs and attempt the pop-up on the waves then I can get to work?"

"I can surf without you." I swallowed.

"No, you need to have someone with you when you're a beginner."

"Right. Okay. I'll head out." I picked up the surfboard by the nose and dragged it into the water.

"Remember everything I've taught you the last few weeks," Nate called to my back.

"Right." I dipped my head, totally confused by Nate's behavior.

Once in the water, I turned my concentration to the waves and everything Nate had taught me about surfing. I needed to do this today, so I'd put a smile back on his face. I paddled out deeper and waited.

Sucking in a deep breath, I paddled into the wave. Placing my hands on the deck, I popped up and stood. I held my arms out for balance as the power of the wave washed me into shore. This was it. I was surfing...I wobbled...and fell into the water with a splash. I broke the surface and clambered back onto my board.

So close.

Nate waved at me from shore. I gave him a thumbs-up and paddled back out.

I can do this.

The next wave surged. I said a silent plea to get it right and paddled into the wave. This time I didn't wobble. I rode the wave like a pro, well, like a pro beginner. I grinned in delight and raced up the sand to a waiting Nate.

There was a smile on his face.

"I did it!"

"You did." He grinned. "I knew you would."

"Thank you, Nate, you don't know what it means for you to teach me." I brushed back my damp hair.

He opened his mouth and shut it again. Then slid his sunglasses onto his face even though no sunshine broke through the mass of clouds.

"I can't believe I surfed a wave," I babbled. "It's amazing. No wonder you surfed for a career."

Nate turned from me. "I should get to work before the storm comes."

"Yes, sorry."

We walked up the beach together.

"I won't have time to stop for lunch today."

"Oh, okay." My stomach dropped.

"I start a new job tomorrow. I won't have time for a surf lesson in the morning."

This was it. Nate would finish working on my house today, he'd finished teaching me how to surf, and I'd never see him again.

"Sure, no problem," I croaked. Tears stung my eyes. I raced up the stairs of the deck and left the board outside.

I fled to the shower where I let the idiotic tears fall. What did I expect? We weren't anything other than employer and employee, teacher and student. Now that it was all finished, we were too.

After submitting the divorce papers, I stopped at Hannah's house. I couldn't stand being in my house and catching glimpses of Nate knowing I'd never see him again after today. And when my divorce was almost final too. I'd imagined telling him today but after this morning, Garry signing the papers wouldn't mean anything to him. Yet, it meant a lot to me. My divorce gave me hope for more between us. Idiot.

Hannah poured me a cup of tea and studied me with a worried expression.

"Want to tell me?"

"No." I nursed the cup.

Bosco jumped onto the lounge and wedged himself between me and Hannah. I patted his soft, velvety ears while he gazed up with his big, brown eyes.

"I should get a dog."

"A dog?" Hannah spluttered.

"You seem happy with just a dog. Men are too complicated."

Hannah patted Bosco's head, and he turned his eyes her way.

"Dogs are an excellent company, but I'd much prefer a man."

"Really?"

"Yes. I know I've not dated much, since... but..." She shrugged. "I want to experience love as I write about it. Don't you?"

"I'm not sure it exists."

"I am."

"How? How do you keep hoping for unconditional love when you've never had it?" I placed the cup on the coffee table.

"Because I've seen love so many times here in Hope Bay."

I sniggered. "Hope Bay or Lover's Bay?"

"Now there's an idea for a book." She tapped her chin.

"How is your new book going?"

"Exceptionally well. I've used a certain Hope Bay couple for inspiration."

"Did you ask their permission first?"

"Don't need to. She's my sister and won't mind."

"What?" I babbled. "Me? Inspiration? I'm not in a couple."

"Aren't you?"

"No, I'm not. Garry signed the divorce papers today. I'm officially a non-couple. Well, once the court approves them."

"I don't mean Garry, and about bloody time."

"What are you talking about then?"

"Nate."

I scowled. "Nate? He's nothing."

"Isn't he?"

"No, he's finishing work today and then I'll never see him again."

"Did he say that?"

"Not in so many words, but it's what he hinted at."

"You're wrong, Madeline."

"How am I wrong? He said he didn't want to have lunch with me today, and he wouldn't have time for a surfing lesson tomorrow. I'd say it was his way of telling me he wouldn't be back."

"It could be. But what if..."

"No." I cut her off. "He was distant this morning. Nothing like his usual warm and friendly self."

"Did something upset him?"

"I don't know. He's always so happy. Even when he's worried about Oliver but Oliver is ecstatic about his new job. So that can't be it."

"What did you do to upset him?"

"Me?" I squawked.

"Yeah, you. He has the hots for you."

"He does not."

"Does too. Otherwise, why would he spend so much time with you?"

"You're wrong. He's just nice, and I was late for my surf lesson today because of Garry—oh—Garry."

"What about Garry?"

"What if he caught sight of me with Garry? And thought..."

"Thought what?"

"I hugged Garry goodbye. What if he assumed it was something else?"

"Madeline," Hannah groaned.

I shifted to the edge of the lounge. My body wanted to go to him. I should tell Nate about the hug, but after this morning, would he care? If I'd imagined our connection... I slumped against the cushions.

"What are you doing?" she screeched. "Get up and go tell him."

I jolted upright at her shrill voice.

"I can't."

"You can." She shoved my back. "You want to. You like him. Go get him."

"But he's younger than me." I swatted at her hand.

"A few years doesn't matter." She smacked my hand back.

"But what if he doesn't like me that way?"

She grabbed my hand. "What if he does? What if this is your chance at love? Do you want to live your life wondering? Or do you want to take a chance at finding love?"

I searched her face recalling all the times I'd spent with Nate, the fun, the laughter, the teasing, and the happiness in his presence. Did I want to let him go? Or never see him again?

No.

I jumped up from the lounge.

"There's my amazing sister." Hannah stood with me. "Go get him."

I rushed from Hannah's house and outside to mine. I ran a loop of my property trying to find Nate but didn't find him. Where was he? I skidded to a stop in the front yard. His truck was absent from the driveway. He'd left already.

The sky darkened with heavy grey clouds, like my mood.

Was it a sign I shouldn't tell him how I felt? What if there isn't more between us and I should leave things as they are?

A bolt of lightning zapped across the dark sky. Another sign I should tell him because every time he touched me it felt like a zap of electricity running between us.

What did I have to lose?

Besides, I'd never hear the end of it from Hannah.

I hurried inside and grabbed my car keys. He shouldn't be far. He couldn't have left long ago. I should be able to catch him.

I could ring him.

But I wanted to see his face and his smile. I wanted to be the one to make him smile. I wanted to kiss his lips and run my hands over the muscles I'd gazed at with admiration for so many weeks.

And I wanted to tell him. Tell him what?

Tell him I liked him.

Idiotic. How old am I?

I should tell him I'd developed feelings for him.

Yes, that's better.

Feelings that one day might be the ultimate love.

Hannah's right. I wanted the love she wrote about.

Who didn't?

Chapter Sixteen

I should tell him I'd never be a good mother to his...

Yes, that's better.

Each has their one day: might he the ultimate love

Hannah might be want the love she wrote about.

Why didn't...

F at drops of rain hit the windshield in a hard splatter. I turned on the wipers and swished them away trying to let my doubts swish away too. Nate's truck was nowhere in sight on the road, and I didn't know where he was. I should pull over and called him, but a force inside me urged me to head to his house.

Fifteen minutes later I parked in front of his beach house.

Nerves suddenly made my palms damp and my heart race to the beat of the driving rain.

To get out of the car and knock on the door or head home?

Hannah would scold me if I chickened out when I was this close.

I jumped out of the car and slammed the door. The big raindrops pelted me. The refreshing scent of new rain reminded me this was a new me. I ran up to the front door and knocked. Moments later, which felt like an eternity, the door opened, and Nate's familiar smiling face greeted me.

"Madeline," he exclaimed. "Come in before you get soaked."

I stepped inside his house suddenly questioning why I was here. Why did I imagine there was more to our time together?

"I'm sorry. I should go," I said.

Nate wiped the drops of rain running down my forehead before they fell into my eyes. I gazed up at him. The butterflies took flight in my stomach.

"Stay. It's not good driving weather."

A loud crack of thunder erupted. I jumped and landed closer to Nate. He lifted his hands and placed them on my shoulders. A tremble took up residence.

"Don't you like storms?"

"It's not the storm." I pushed my damp hair back and tucked the strands behind my ear.

"I'll get you a towel." He let go of my shoulders and left me standing in his hallway. Then he turned. "Are you coming?"

I trailed after him along the long hallway. Nate turned into the bathroom, and I followed him, taking in the clean white and blue tiles of the room. They fit with his beach house. He lifted a thick navy blue towel from the handrail and passed it to me. I wiped my face and arms then patted my hair. Nate watched me with a quietness that sat like lead in my stomach instead of the butterflies I was used to fluttering in his presence.

"Thanks." I handed him the towel.

"Are you cold? I can get you something else to wear if you like."

"No. I'm good." I was hot with working up the courage to tell Nate everything, and the muggy air with the rain in the summer's heat didn't help.

"Why are you here?"

"Oh, I, ah." I was an idiot. He didn't want me here. I lifted my hands to my cheeks willing myself to not blush.

Nate's gaze landed on my left hand and his eyebrows rose. He traced the tan line on my ring finger.

"You've taken off your wedding ring."

"Yes," I whispered.

He stepped closer and then stopped.

"Let's have a drink to celebrate on the deck and watch the storm."

"I'd like that."

He dropped his hand, and I trailed after him. He paused in his kitchen with woodgrain countertops and navy-blue cupboards to pour two glasses of wine then he slid open the large sliding glass door. The rain pelted the tin roof of his veranda and echoed the pounding in my head. We stepped outside under the warm and cozy timber-clad veranda scattered with outdoor beanbags. They looked so inviting to sit and watch the storm, but I was too nervous to sit. Too nervous to do anything but clutch my wineglass in a tight fist.

"To your divorce." He clinked his wineglass to mine.

"To my divorce. Well, soon-to-be divorce. The papers have to go through the system, but it should only take a month." I smiled and drank. It felt good, like a cleansing of some sort, toasting to my divorce and washing the aftertaste from my mouth. "I wanted to tell you this morning."

"But then I was a jerk."

"No, you weren't."

"I was, and I'm sorry, Maddy. I tried to figure out a way to stay in your life when I'd completed the job, and you no longer needed surfing lessons. Then I saw you in your kitchen and I assumed you didn't want me to stay as your friend, and possibly more."

I placed my wineglass on the small table next to the nearest beanbag. A bolt of lightning lit up the sky with a blue flare and thunder rumbled in its wake. "That's why I drove here. I like you. Since you appeared in my life, you've shown me what I'm missing, and I don't want to lose it."

"You like me as a friend." He placed his glass next to mine.

"I do."

Another bolt of lightning lit up the sky with a tinge of violet this time followed by the loudest crack of thunder I'd ever heard. The view of the storm over the ocean was like nothing I'd ever seen. Much like my feelings for Nate, they weren't something I'd ever experienced before.

"Nate," I said his name with all those feelings bubbling up in me.

He turned my way. What did I have to lose? I launched myself toward him. Grabbed his face in my hands and kissed his lips hard. His hands gripped my waist keeping me in place as his lips smiled underneath mine. Then he tugged me closer until our bodies pressed tight and deepened the kiss.

Lightning and thunder exploded, not from the sky, but from within me. Nate's kiss was everything I'd imagined from the moment he said he wanted to kiss me. From the moment I'd opened my eyes when he'd rescued me and deemed him the most gorgeous man ever.

We stopped kissing and smiled at each other.

"More than friends," I said. "If that's what you want."

He chuckled. "I don't kiss my friends like that."

"Thank goodness." I sighed and dropped my hands to his chest. "I've never felt like such an idiot than when I'm around you."

"Ah, is that a compliment?"

"It is. You make me feel alive and like anything is possible."

"Anything is possible." He kissed my forehead. "Can I take you on a date tomorrow night?"

"What about tonight?" I trailed my hand down his chest.

He sucked in a breath and caught my hand in his. I leaned into him and kissed him again, emboldened by my feelings for Nate and the fact he felt the same way.

"You said anything is possible," I whispered against his lips.

"I did." He nibbled on my bottom lip. "Didn't I?"

"Mm-hmm." My legs wobbled when the butterflies danced in victory.

Tonight, tomorrow, wherever Nate and my relationship took us, anything was possible.

He lowered his head to my lips and kissed me again. His tongue danced with mine drowning out the pounding of my heartbeat and the sound of the thunder. There was only him and me. His lips were on mine. My lips were on his.

"Maddy," he groaned.

All my life I'd hated the nickname but having it roll from Nate's tongue warmed my insides even more.

He stopped kissing me and asked, "Where would you like me to take you?"

I pressed a kiss to his lips. "I don't want to go anywhere."

"But I thought we agreed on a date."

"Mmm." I pressed a kiss to his lips again. "Haven't our lunches kind of been dates the last few weeks?"

"Good point. I've never had lunch with any of my other clients. Only you, Maddy." His tongue parted my lips and tangled with mine again.

We came up for air minutes later, our chests heaving against each other's.

"It's been weeks of dating then," I said. "I haven't dated in a very long time, but after this many dates, wouldn't we..."

"Madeline, are you trying to seduce me into bed?"

My cheeks heated. No doubt I was a beetroot.

His calloused hands cupped my cheeks.

"I adore the way you blush," he said. "I was about to seduce you."

He held my face as he kissed me with all the pent-up attraction we'd been trying to ignore for weeks. I slid my hands under his T-shirt and groaned at the sensation of his skin against my palms. Not to be outdone, Nate's hands slid under my top and cupped my breast. His thumb swiped over my nipple making my knees tremble with the intensity of the arousal now building between my legs.

Nate shuffled backward and lowered us onto a beanbag. The beans squished under his back as I fell onto his firm body. Now I felt every hard muscle and in particular the one between our bodies. I rolled my hips against his hard length desperate to ease the ache he'd ignited inside me since the moment we'd met.

His hands roamed down my back and followed the curves of my hips. I lifted my head and met the heated green gaze of his eyes. He made me feel invincible. As though I was the only woman in the world he desired. I'd never had a man look at me that way. Every day with Nate had grown those feelings of instant attraction into more.

"Are you sure?" he asked.

I nodded. "You see me for me."

"I can't believe you're here." He stroked a hand through my hair. "I've been dreaming about this since the day we met."

"Me too if I'm honest."

He slid his hands under my top and I lifted my arms over my head. His gaze heated even hotter, as his fingers slipped to the buckle of my bra and released the strap. The warm, sultry air hit my naked breasts, but Nate leaned forward and enclosed one nipple and then the other with his mouth. I sank my fingers into his hair and cried out at the shot of pleasure shooting to my core as his beard stroked the sensitive skin on my chest.

"More," he said. "I want to see you come undone."

This man, and the way he made me feel.

He rolled us over until he was on top, then he pressed a kiss to my quivering stomach and pulled my pants and underwear down in a swift move that left me naked under the stormy night sky. His finger stroked every inch of my skin before sinking into the warmth of my body. Nate dropped his head to the crook of my neck.

"I probably don't deserve someone as good as you, but I want you."

I stroked a hand over his hair. "You deserve goodness in your life, too."

His lips met mine in a soul rendering kiss. Deep inside his fingers stroked nerve endings until my legs trembled and my fingers dug into his hair as I hung onto the building tsunami inside my body.

"Nate," I moaned.

I shattered into a thousand lightning pieces. The orgasm shook me to my core.

"You are so beautiful," Nate whispered. "We don't have to do more."

"I want all of you, Nate."

He stood and stared at me in wonder as he stripped his clothes. Every inch of his bronzed muscles glowed under the lightning strikes in the sky. More lightning lit up my body. My insides clenched with the need to have his firm body against mine. Inside mine. He fished for a condom from his wallet and rolled it on his hard length.

"Next time, I want to do that," I blurted out.

Nate chuckled. "Anything for you."

He lowered himself on top of me. I lifted my legs and wrapped them around his waist. The head of his cock brushed against my slick entrance igniting the nerve endings into a frenzy once more. He held my gaze with his as he slid deep inside me with one roll of his hips.

"Maddy," he groaned.

"Yes," I gasped out.

The way my body felt with his inside mine was so right. So perfect. Our hips moved in sync. Everything fell away except the connection we'd built between us. The connection we'd continue to build. What we felt for each other was more than lust and attraction. We respected each other.

Admired each other.

And maybe more.

Our orgasms came together rocking our bodies to the very core. Each quiver of release made me fall even more for Nate. Deep inside my body, a sense of peace surrounded me. Nate gathered me in his arms and rolled us to the side and cuddled me in the strength of his arms.

"Tomorrow," Nate said, brushing the hair back from my face, "I'm taking you on a proper date."

"Yeah?"

"Dinner, dancing, then my bed."

"I like the sound of that." I snuggled closer to his chest. "But we did all right in the beanbag."

Nate's chest bounced beneath my head as he chuckled. "We did more than all right."

"Who knew beanbags were comfortable for sex?"

Nate's laughter grew and I loved that I was the one to make him happy. In such a short time he'd made me happy too.

As the stormy sky lit up with a bright display of blue and violet lightning, the boom of thunder rolled, and the steady pound of rain tinkled on the rooftop, Nate and I discovered a lot of things were possible if you let yourself believe.

Chapter Seventeen

A month later, I flung open my front door to a smiling, happy Nate. The butterflies in my stomach fluttered in happiness, but I was too nervous to pay them any heed.

"Look what I picked up." Nate lifted his hands full of shopping bags.

"I can't. I'm too nervous."

Nate walked inside and dropped a kiss on my forehead. "You've got nothing to worry about."

I shut the door behind him and Sampson. "But what if my first guests give me a dreadful review?"

"They won't. This beach house is great, and you're amazing. They'll love it here." He headed to the kitchen.

I trailed after him, more nervous about my opening day than I considered I would be. What if it was a disaster? What if they didn't like me? Or the house? What if the food turned out terrible? No, that wouldn't happen. Oliver was helping cook dinner tonight for the guests. I relaxed a fraction. I wanted everything to go smoothly, and for my first guests to enjoy the beach house as much as I did.

Nate placed the bags on the counter and opened one. "I have opening-day gifts."

"Really?" Emotion clogged my throat.

"Yep, sweets." He withdrew a smaller bag with the Blissful Bites logo and placed it in the fridge. "For later."

I pouted. I could do with a boost of sugar right about now. Something to take my mind off the guests arriving tonight.

He withdrew the next item.

"You bought my favorite wine?"

"Yep, for later too." He placed the bottle of pink Moscato in the fridge too. "We'll toast your success on the deck tonight."

I folded my arms. "How are they opening-day gifts if I can't have them yet?" Even though wine on the deck with Nate sounded perfect. And romantic like the other nights we'd snuggled on the deck on the bench seats he'd built, under the stars, with the sound of the surf playing us its love song.

Nate chuckled and withdrew the next item.

I gasped.

He laid the wooden sign on the counter. The words "Madeline's Guest House" were emblazoned in black across the white-painted timber.

"Oh, Nate, it's perfect. You're perfect."

"You can hang the sign out the front for your guests to see."

I rounded the counter and threw my arms around his neck.

He smiled with such happiness, the lines around his eyes danced. All my emotions bubbled to the surface. The butterflies in my stomach danced with love. I gazed into his eyes. This moment here was perfect for me to tell him.

I smiled with all the happiness he'd brought me. "I love you."

Nate eased me closer. "I love you too."

I kissed him with the love he'd given me. The love I'd always imagined was possible but never experienced until Nate. My nerves about the opening day for the bed-and-breakfast were the last thing on my mind.

Nate rustled the sheets back and slid out of bed. I tugged the sheets over my body and ogled his sexy body as he stepped into his boxer shorts.

"Where are you going?"

"To the kitchen. I'm hungry."

"You're always hungry," I joked.

"Hungry for you." He strode back to the bed and kissed me with all the passion and love I held for him.

Nate grinned, the smile lines I adored so much lighting his face. He disappeared from the room and walked back carrying two paper bags. As I lifted the sheets, he slid under and handed me a bag.

"What's this?" I peered inside. "Is it?"

"Yep." He smiled.

"No way." I rustled the bag until its contents peeked out the top. "Bailey's custard slice."

"It is Friday."

"Why are you so perfect?" I snuggled into his side and bit into the sweet custard slice.

Barking keened and the thunder of the dog's paws on the timber floors traveled closer to the bedroom.

"You forgot to shut the door." I pointed at the door.

Bosco and Sampson ran into the room and jumped on the bed before Nate stirred.

"Get down," Nate scolded and pointed at the floor.

Sampson obeyed, but Bosco clambered over me. He lunged for the custard slice. I held him back with my free hand.

"Bosco," I scolded and lost my grip on him. I jerked the custard slice away and smeared custard across my cheek. Nate rescued me, again, before I ended up more of a mess. He lugged Bosco from the bedroom and firmly shut the door.

"That dog." He shook his head.

"Hannah wanted to be here with her writer friends. I couldn't say no since she made my opening weekend a success."

"She only lives next door. Bosco should have stayed there," Nate grumbled.

"Leave him be. If Bosco hadn't caused such a catastrophe the day we met, who knows, maybe we wouldn't have fallen in love."

Nate crawled back into bed, his custard slice forgotten on the bedside table.

"I wanted to lick the custard slice from your face the day we met," he said. "I guess I can this time."

"That'd be inappropriate." I traced the tattoo on his bicep with my fingers.

"Totally." He grinned then swiped his tongue across my cheek.

I giggled. Seriously giggled. The happiest I'd ever been in my life.

Read more Hope Bay stories
Falling For Mr. Fake It

Free book

Would you like to read Katie and Joel's story?
Download your free ebook Finding Love with Mr. Perfect.
https://BookHip.com/GMZMGTW

Afterword

Did you love my story?

A reader who writes a review for a book is a tremendous gift to the author. It lets me know that someone read my book and enjoyed the story enough to tell me. If you enjoyed this book, please leave a review I'd be forever grateful.

Acknowledgments

First, thank you to my family for putting up with me disappearing into the world of books. A special thank you to my daughter Sarah for designing my beautiful covers. To Belinda, thank you for encouraging me to write again after I lost everything in a computer crash. Remember to back up! A lot of work goes into creating a story, and I'm always thankful for the support of my online writing buddies, beta readers, and fellow authors, Immy for always making me smile, Tammy for believing in me from the start, Karen for being willing to read any level of heat I write, Cassie for her hand holding, Lana for her invaluable knowledge. The biggest thank you goes to my 'twin' Dannielle, who is the best critique partner, cheerleader, and sounding board ever, and is forever fixing my comma errors, sorry Dannielle I'm afraid you're stuck with them and me. Finally thank you to all you romance readers. You are my tribe.

About Author

Helen Walton is a tea drinking, chocoholic, romance writer. Stories are her obsession. She adores creating sensual romances containing a sprinkling of humor and the all-important happy ending. She lives in South Australia with her family, and menagerie of quirky animals where they all take her away from her book world and demand to be fed. Lucky for them, she enjoys cooking but prefers baking.

Sign up for my newsletter for exclusive content.

https://www.helenwaltonauthor.com/newsletter

Visit my website

https://www.helenwaltonauthor.com/

Follow me

BB   bookbub.com/profile/helen-walton

f   facebook.com/Helen-Walton-Author-103496667706602/

g   goodreads.com/author/show/20249188.Helen_Walton

instagram.com/helen.walton.author

tiktok.com/@helen.walton.author

Also By

His Pleasure Contract

Love Negotiations

Her Love Submission

Hollywood Hearts Short Stories

How The Grinch Lusted After Santa

Lusting After Valentine

The Lustful Leprechaun

The Lust Bunny

Lustman To The Rescue

The Lust Giving

Anthologies

Reluctant Bride

Alpha Male